"Gran gave each o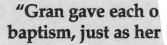
baptism, just as her said.

Luke stood, and he was very close to her. "What's your verse, Chloe?" His blue eyes seemed to darken, staring into hers with such intensity that she couldn't escape.

"It's from Jeremiah. 'For I know the plans I have for you,' says the Lord. 'Plans to prosper you and not to harm you. Plans to give you hope and a future.'"

"Hope and a future," he repeated softly. "That's a nice promise, Chloe Elizabeth." He hugged her, his cheek warm against hers as if they really were the couple her family believed them to be.

She could only nod. It had been a mistake to bring Luke Hunter here. She should have known that it would be. Things had changed between them. They'd never be the same again.

And he couldn't know, not ever, that she longed for this to be real.

Books by Marta Perry

Love Inspired

A Father's Promise #41
Since You've Been Gone #75
*Desperately Seeking Daddy #91
*The Doctor Next Door #104
*Father Most Blessed #128
A Father's Place #153
Hunter's Bride #172

*Hometown Heroes

MARTA PERRY

began writing children's stories for Sunday school take-home papers while she was a church educational director. From that beginning she branched into writing magazine fiction and then book-length fiction. She's grateful for the opportunity to write the kind of books she loves to read.

Marta lives in rural Pennsylvania with her husband of thirty-seven years and has three grown children they enjoy visiting, scattered around the globe. In addition to writing and travel, Marta loves hearing from readers and enjoys responding to their letters. She can be reached c/o Steeple Hill Books, 300 East 42nd Street, New York, NY 10017.

Hunter's Bride
Marta Perry

Love Inspired®

Published by Steeple Hill Books™

STEEPLE HILL BOOKS

Steeple
Hill™

ISBN 0-373-87179-1

HUNTER'S BRIDE

Copyright © 2002 by Martha Johnson

Visit us at www.steeplehill.com

Printed in U.S.A.

For I know the plans I have for you, says the Lord.
Plans to prosper you and not to harm you.
Plans to give you hope and a future.
—*Jeremiah* 29:11

This story is dedicated with much love
to my daughter Lorie, my son-in-law Axel,
and especially to my grandson, Bjoern Jacob.

And, as always, to Brian.

Chapter One

Chloe Caldwell was in trouble—deep, deep trouble. She tried to stand up straight against the intense, ice-blue stare of her boss, Luke Hunter. He wore the look some of his business rivals had compared to being pierced by a laser. She began to understand the feeling.

Southern women have skin like magnolia blossoms and spines like steel. Gran's voice echoed in her mind. *Have you lost yourself up north among them Yankees, Chloe Elizabeth?*

Maybe she had. She took a strained breath and met Luke's gaze. "I don't know what you mean."

He arched his black eyebrows. "It's a simple question, Chloe." He held up a sheet of off-white note-paper covered with spidery handwriting. "Why does your grandmother think you and I are a couple?"

Possibly, if she closed her eyes, she'd open them

to find this was all a dream—no, a nightmare. *Oh, Gran,* she thought despairingly, *whatever possessed you to write to him?* Luke must have picked up the mail when she'd been out of the office for a few minutes. If she'd seen it— But she hadn't.

Luke was waiting for an answer, and no one had ever accused Luke Hunter of an abundance of patience. She had to say something.

"I can't imagine." *Liar,* the voice of her conscience whispered. "May I see the letter?"

She held out her hand, trying to find enough of that steel Gran insisted she had so that her fingers wouldn't tremble and give her away. Luke held the paper just out of her reach for a moment, like a cat toying with a mouse, and then surrendered it. He leaned back against the polished oak desk that the Dalton Resorts considered appropriate for a rising executive. He should have looked relaxed. He didn't.

She shot a hopeful glance toward the telephone. It rang all day long. Why not now? But the phone remained stubbornly silent. Beyond the desk, large windows looked out on a gray March day in Chicago, an even grayer Lake Michigan. No sudden tornado swept down to rip the sheet from her hand.

She forced her attention to Gran's letter. She'd barely begun to decipher the old-fashioned handwriting, when Luke moved restlessly, drawing her gaze inevitably back to him.

She'd long ago realized that Luke Hunter was a study in contradictions. Night-black hair and eyebrows that were another slash of black contrasted with incredibly deep blue eyes. The strong bones of cheek and jaw reflected his fierce tenacity, but the impression was tempered by the unexpected widow's peak on his forehead and the cleft in his chin.

It didn't take one of Gran's homegrown country philosophies to tell her what to think of Luke. A man with a face like that had secrets to hide. He wore the smooth, polished exterior that announced a rising young executive, but underneath was something darker, something that ran against the grain. She'd been his good right arm for nearly six years and had never seen more than a hint of it, but she knew it was there.

She took a breath. "I'm sorry that you received this." The paper fluttered in her grasp. "I don't know why Gran decided to send you an invitation to her eightieth birthday party next Sunday."

"Oh, she says why." Luke leaned forward, invading her space. "She thinks I'm your 'beau.'" His tone put quotes around a word she'd never expected to hear from him. "Why does she think that?"

"My grandmother is an elderly lady." She would try to convey the image of someone frail and confused, while sending a fervent mental apology to her peppery Gran. No one who knew Naomi Caldwell would dare to call her frail or confused.

"She sounds pretty coherent to me." He plucked the letter back from her, and she had to fight to keep from snatching it. "If she thinks that, it must be because someone gave her that idea."

Please, Lord.

She stopped the prayer before it could become any more self-serving than it already was. Obviously no heavenly intervention was going to excuse her from the results of her own folly.

"I'm afraid I must have." She picked her way through the words carefully, as if she were back on the island, picking her way through the marsh grasses. "I think it happened when you gave me those symphony tickets. When I told her about it, she misunderstood. She assumed we went together."

"And you didn't correct her?"

She felt color warm her cheeks. "I thought..." *Well, that sentence was going nowhere. Try again.* "My grandmother worries about me. You have to realize she's never been farther from home than Savannah. Chicago is another world to her. Once she thought I was dating someone safe, she stopped worrying so much."

His eyebrows lifted. "Am I safe, Chloe?"

She'd stepped in a bog without seeing it. "I mean, someone she'd heard of. Naturally, I've often spoken of my boss." Probably more than she should have. "I didn't tell her any lies. I just...didn't clear things up." It was time to get out of this situation with what remaining dignity she had. "I'm sorry you were bothered with this. Naturally, I'll tell her you won't be coming to Caldwell Cove."

Luke looked again at the letter, with some sharpening of attention she didn't understand.

"That's in South Carolina, isn't it?"

She nodded. "It's on Caldwell Island, just off the coast."

"Caldwell Cove, Caldwell Island. Sounds as if you belong there, Chloe."

The faint trace of mockery in his voice made her stiffen. "I belong *here* now."

"Still, to have a whole island named after you must mean something."

"It only means that my ancestors were the first settlers. They gave their name to the village and to the island. It doesn't mean every descendant stays put." *She* hadn't.

She held out her hand, hoping he'd give her that embarrassing missive so she could destroy it. "Again, I'm sorry."

But he turned away, dropping the letter onto his desk. He glanced back at her, amusement in his eyes. "I'm not. It's been an interesting break in the routine."

"Speaking of which—" She looked at her watch. "You have a meeting with Mr. Dalton at eleven."

"No." The amusement disappeared from his face. "He was in early and he talked with me then."

It went without saying that Luke had been in early. She sometimes wondered when he slept. "I see. Are there any meeting notes I should take care of?"

"None." His voice contained an edge. "Just get me the Branson file, that's all."

He moved effortlessly back to Dalton Resorts business, obviously dismissing her and her small problems from his mind. She could escape. She'd reached the door when his voice stopped her.

"Chloe."

"Yes?" She turned back reluctantly.

"Too bad I won't be seeing Caldwell Cove. It might have been fun at that."

Fun? She tried to imagine Luke Hunter, urban to the soles of his handmade Italian shoes, in Caldwell Cove. No, she didn't think that would have been fun for anyone, least of all her. She gave him a meaningless smile and scurried out the door.

Once safely behind her desk, she took a deep breath, trying to quell the flood of embarrassment. *It's your own fault,* the voice of her conscience said sternly, sounding remarkably like her grandmother. *You set this in motion with your fairy tales.*

Fairy tales, that's all they'd been—innocent fairy tales. Letting Gran believe she and Luke Hunter were a couple had let her believe it, too, for a time. She shied away from that thought.

She should have realized that sooner or later this would backfire. She pressed her fingers to her temples, trying to erase the pounding that had begun there. She'd known he'd never give up until he had the whole story. That tenacity of Luke's had played a major role in his success at Dalton Resorts.

She'd seen that quality when she first met him, when she came to Chicago six years ago. His office had been the size of a broom closet then, and she'd been the greenest member of the secretarial pool, homesick for the island and trying to find her way through the maze of corporate politics.

She'd learned fast, though probably not as fast as he had. She'd discovered that she had to get rid of her soft Southern drawl if she didn't want to be made fun of. She'd found that there were as many alligators in the corporate structure as she'd ever seen in the lagoons on the island. And she'd realized that if you wanted to survive, you attached yourself to a rising star.

That star had been Luke Hunter, with his newly minted MBA and his fierce, aggressive intelligence. They'd come up together, working long hours, until they'd become a team, almost able to read each other's thoughts. She'd identified herself with his interests, and she'd never regretted that move. Until, possibly, today, when her two worlds had collided.

She looked at the framed family photo on her desk, and warmth slipped through her. The Caldwell kin, everyone from Gran to little Sammy, aunts, uncles, brothers, cousins, even second cousins twice removed, had gathered on the dock for that picture. It was a wonder the weathered wooden structure hadn't collapsed. She could still smell the salt tang in the air, feel the hot sun on her shoulders and the warm boards beneath her bare feet, hear the soft Southern voices teasing.

She'd told Luke she belonged here now, but she wasn't sure that was true. She'd made friends, found a church home, learned her way around, but she'd never developed that sophisticated urban manner her friends wore so easily. Maybe the truth was, she was trapped between her two worlds, and she wasn't sure which one claimed her.

But Luke Hunter didn't need to know that. Any more than he needed to know the real reason she'd let Gran believe she was dating him. Not for Gran's sake, but for her own.

You've got a crush on that corporate shark. She could still hear the incredulity in her friend Marsha's voice when she'd let her secret slip. *Girl, are you crazy? That man could eat you alive.*

Chloe hadn't been able to explain, but she hadn't been able to deny it, either. Marsha hadn't seen the side of the man that Luke sometimes showed her.

Chloe traced the family photo with one finger. When the call had come two years earlier about her father's accident, it had been Luke who'd taken control in that nightmare moment. She'd been almost too stunned to function at the thought of her strong, vibrant father, the rock they all depended upon, lying still and white in a hospital bed.

Luke had arranged her flight home, he'd driven her to the airport, then he'd stayed with her until the Flight was called. He'd even watered the plants on her desk while she was gone. He'd never questioned her need to stay on the island until Daddy was on his feet again.

No, Marsha didn't understand that. All the same, she'd been right. Chloe Caldwell did indeed have one giant-size crush on her boss.

Luke spun his chair around to stare out at the city. His city. Having a window big enough to look at it meant he was on the verge of success.

Or failure. The brief skirmish with Chloe had diverted his attention from the problem at hand, but now that situation drove back at him like a semi barreling down the interstate. Chloe had innocently mentioned the meeting with Dalton. She couldn't have known just what kind of bomb Leonard Dalton had set ticking this morning.

A vice-presidency was in the offing, and the CEO had laid it out very clearly. Luke could prove he was ready by finding the ideal location for the next Dalton Resort and negotiating a favorable deal. If not—

Luke's hand formed a fist. Opportunity didn't knock all that often. He intended to answer the first time. He'd come too far, and he wasn't going to be denied the reward for all his effort.

His mind took a reluctant sidelong glance at just how far he'd come. He didn't let himself look often, because that was looking into a black hole of poverty, ugliness, rejection—a hole that might suck you back in if you looked too long.

He forced the image away by sheer willpower. No one in his current life knew about his past, and no one would. He'd be the next vice-president, because he wouldn't accept anything else. And Chloe, quite without meaning to, might have given him the key.

Amusement filtered through him. That must have been the first time he'd seen Chloe Caldwell—quiet, composed, efficient Chloe—embarrassed by something.

Well, however embarrassing Chloe had found the exposure of her little fib, he'd have to thank her for it, because the mention of Caldwell Island, South Carolina, had rung a bell in his memory. He spun back to the computer and flicked through the past several years of site survey reports.

There it was. The area surrounding Caldwell Island had appeared on a list of possible sites for a new Dalton Resort three years ago. Dalton hadn't established a new resort at that time, and this report had quietly vanished. He might be the only one in the company who remembered Caldwell Island.

He skimmed through the report quickly, his excitement mounting. Something—the little vibration he'd learned to trust—told him this was worth pursuing.

He leaned back, smiling. One of the hardest things about looking over a possible site was keeping the locals from learning what you were doing and thus sending prices soaring. Chloe, with her sweet little deception and the frail old grandmother she wouldn't want to disappoint, had just given him the perfect way to check out Caldwell Island for himself.

Chloe hadn't had enough time to forget her humiliation when the buzzer summoned her, insistent as an angry mosquito. Snatching a pad, she marched toward Luke's office. All right, there was to be no reprieve. She'd go in there and show Luke that they were back to business, as if the morning's fiasco had never happened.

"Chloe." He looked up from a file on his desk. "I was thinking about that letter from your grandmother."

All right, she wouldn't be able to pretend it hadn't happened. *Steel, Chloe Elizabeth.*

"Please forget about it. I'll take care of it." She raised the pad. "Was there something else you wanted?"

"I can't forget about it." He leaned back in the padded executive chair. Beyond him, gray rain slashed against the window, as relentless as he was. "I keep picturing your frail old grandmother being disappointed on her birthday."

Wouldn't he be surprised by the real Gran, one of a long line of strong Caldwell women who'd wrestle a gator if necessary to keep her family safe. "Gran will be fine." She tried to put a little of that strength into her voice. "After all, the rest of her kin will be there."

The word slipped out before she could censor it.

Northerners didn't call people "kin." She'd been thinking too much about Gran today.

"But not her favorite granddaughter." He smiled. "I'm sure you are the favorite, aren't you?"

Warning bells began to ring. When Luke turned on the charm, he wanted something. "That's probably my sister, Miranda. After all, she's produced a great-grandchild."

Luke swung forward in his chair, his feet landing on the carpet. "In any event, she'd be disappointed. I just can't let that happen."

She stared at him blankly, not sure where he was going with this. "I don't..."

"Besides, what is it to us? One short weekend out of our lives to make an elderly lady happy."

Panic rocketed through her. He couldn't be saying what she thought he was.

"You can't be talking about going." Her voice rose in spite of herself.

He stood, planting both hands on the desktop and leaning toward her. "That would solve everything, wouldn't it?"

"No!"

"Why not?"

Her mind worked frantically. "We can't pretend to be dating in front of my whole family."

"Again, why not?" His words shot toward her, compelling agreement.

Her throat closed on the difficulty of telling him all the reasons. As usual, standing up to Luke Hunter was about as possible for her as flying to the moon. "We just can't, that's all."

"Nonsense. Of course we can." He swept past her objections, and with fascinated horror she saw him launching into the deal mode that no one ever managed to stop. "In fact, I've already done it."

"Done what?" Her thoughts twisted and turned, trying to find a path out of this impossible situation.

"I called and talked with your father." There might have been something a little malicious in his smile. "He was delighted that we're coming. I'll fly down with you on Friday. We'll come back Sunday night after the birthday party."

"But I can't. *We* can't."

"Of course you can. All you have to do is reschedule my Friday meetings and pack, and we'll make your grandmother happy. Aren't you pleased, Chloe?"

Pleased? She could only stare at him, the horrible truth rolling inexorably toward her. Thanks to her weakness for storytelling and her total inability to stand up to Luke Hunter, she was condemned to spend the weekend pretending to her family that he cared for her.

She might have dreamed, in her weaker moments, of going back to Caldwell Cove with Luke on her arm. But this wasn't a dream. It was a nightmare, and yet it was only too real.

Chapter Two

"We're almost there." Chloe leaned forward in the passenger seat next to Luke, sounding as eager as a ten-year-old on a vacation.

"How can you tell? It all looks the same to me." Luke pressed his hands against the steering wheel of the rental car and stretched. The trip to Caldwell Island from the airport in Savannah was less than an hour, but the narrow, two-lane roads wove through apparently endless miles of tall pines alternating with dense, dark undergrowth. It might have made sense for Chloe to drive, since she knew the road, but he hated letting someone else drive him.

He was also starting to have serious doubts about this whole expedition. Nothing he'd seen so far would lead him to consider this area for a Dalton Resort. It looked more like Tobacco Road.

Chloe flashed him a smile. "Just a little farther, and you'll see the bridge."

He'd see it. Then he'd see this precious island of hers. He'd be able to tell in half an hour, probably, if Caldwell Island was worth further investigation. If not, what he'd want to do was take the first plane back to Chicago.

But he couldn't. Like it or not, he'd committed to this weekend, to pretending he and Chloe weren't just boss and secretary, but something more. A faint apprehension trickled along his nerves. Chloe, with her honey-colored hair and her golden-brown eyes, was appealing, but certainly not his type. He went for sophisticated, not girl-next-door. Pulling this off could be tricky.

"There!" Chloe's exclamation was filled with satisfaction as they emerged abruptly from yet another stand of pine trees.

He blinked. Ahead of them, lush grass stretched on either side of the road, golden in the sunshine. It might have been a meadow, but the grass grew in water, not earth. In the distance a cluster of palmettos stood dark against the sky, like an island. Sunlight glinted from deeper streams, turning the scene into a bewildering world between earth and sea. His apprehension deepened. Everything about this was alien to him.

Chloe hit the button, and her window whirred down, letting in a flood of warm air that mixed salt, sea and musky vegetation. "Smell that." She inhaled deeply. "That's what tells me I've come home." She hung out the window, letting her hair tangle in the breeze.

"Doesn't smell like home to me. Not unless it includes exhaust fumes, sidewalk vendors and pigeons."

"Sorry. Would you settle for a great white heron?" She pointed, and he saw an elegant white bird lift its long neck and stare at them.

This was a different Chloe, he realized. One who knew everything here, one who was in her element. Just as he was out of his. The thought made him vaguely uneasy.

The road swept up onto a white bridge, shimmering in the sunshine. Tall pylons marched beside the bridge, feet in the water, carrying power lines.

"We're crossing the inland waterway," Chloe said, pressing her palms against the dash as if to force the car to move faster. "And there's Caldwell Island."

The car crested the hump in the middle of the bridge, and Chloe's island lay ahead of them. His breath caught in spite of himself. The surrounding marsh grass made the island shimmer with gold, and it stretched along the horizon like an early explorer's dream of riches.

"Golden isles," Chloe said softly, as if she read his thought. "That's an old name for the sea islands. The Golden Isles."

The channel merged with marshes, then the

marshes merged with the gentle rise of land, as if the island raised itself only reluctantly from the sea. A village drifted along the curve of shore facing the bridge, looking like something out of the last century, or maybe the century before that. A church steeple bisected it neatly.

The island was beautiful. It was desirable. And unless there was something unexpected out of his sight, it was also completely uncommercialized. Excitement stirred in him.

"What's the ante-bellum mansion? A hotel?"

She glanced toward the far end of the village, then shook her head, smiling. "That's my uncle Jefferson's house. Uncle Jeff's family is the rich branch of the clan. There aren't any hotels on Caldwell Island, just the inn my parents own and a few guest houses."

He didn't want to raise her suspicions, but he risked another comment. "You're not going to tell me vacationers haven't discovered this place."

She seemed too preoccupied to notice, staring out as if cherishing every landmark. "There have always been summer visitors, but they're people who've owned their homes here for generations." She pointed. "Turn left off the bridge. Town's only three streets deep, so you can't get lost. We'll go straight to the inn. They'll be waiting."

He followed her directions, wondering a little at the sureness in her voice. *They'll be waiting.*

He passed a small grocery, a bait shop and then

what seemed to be a boatyard with the Caldwell name emblazoned on its sign. Before he could ask if her family owned it, Chloe spoke again.

"There it is. That's The Dolphin."

The inn sat on their right, facing the waterway, spreading out gracefully under the surrounding trees. The core of the building looked only one room deep, but succeeding generations must have added one wing after another as their families, or their ambitions, grew. Gray shingles blended with the gray-green of the lace-draped live oaks, and rocking chairs dotted a wraparound porch.

"Those are our boats." She pointed to a covey of boats at the dock on their left. "Everyone's in. I told you they'd be waiting for us."

Apparently here they counted boats, instead of cars, to tell them who was where. He drove into a shell-covered driveway and pulled to a stop, discovering a knot of apprehension in his gut.

Ridiculous. He dismissed it quickly. Chloe's family had no reason to suspect him of anything, and their opinions didn't matter to him in the least. Simple country people, that's all they were.

Simple, maybe. But had Chloe warned him there were so many of them? He stepped out of the car into what seemed to be a mob of Caldwells, all talking at once. Chloe was right—they'd been waiting. An unidentifiable breed of half-grown dog bounced around the crowd, its barks adding to the general chaos.

He looked to Chloe for help, but a woman who must be her mother was enveloping her in an enormous hug. A younger woman, with Chloe's heart-shaped face but auburn hair and green eyes, wrapped her arms around both of them. All three seemed to be talking and crying at once.

"Don't suppose we'll get any sense out of those three for a time."

The rangy, sun-bronzed man who held out a large hand was probably about Luke's age. Big—that was his first thought. Luke stood six foot, and this guy had a couple of inches on him at least. The hand that grasped his had power behind it. One of the brothers?

"Guess I'd best do the introductions, since our Chloe's forgotten her manners," he continued. "I'm Daniel. This is David."

Luke blinked. There were two of them. "Chloe didn't mention her brothers were twins." He shook hands with the other giant, trying to assess the differences between them.

There weren't many. Both men were big, both sun-brown, both lean and muscular. They had identical brown eyes and identical sun-bleached hair. David wore a pair of wire-rimmed glasses, apparently the only way Luke would ever tell them apart.

"She wouldn't." Daniel seemed to do the talking for the pair of them. "She always said it wasn't fair there were two of us to gang up on her." He reached out a long arm to pull over a gangly teenager. "This one's Theo. He's the baby."

The boy reddened under his tan, shooting his brother a resentful look before offering his hand to Luke. "Nice to meet you, sir."

"Luke, please."

His effort at friendliness just made the boy's flush deepen. "Yes, sir."

"That's Miranda's boy, Sammy, trying to make his mutt pipe down." Daniel gestured toward a boy of six or so, wrestling with the dog over a stick. "And this is our daddy, Clayton Caldwell."

Luke turned, and his smile stiffened on his face. There could be no doubt of the assessment in the sharp hazel eyes that met his gaze. He was abruptly aware of intelligence, shrewdness, questioning.

"Luke. Welcome to Caldwell Cove." Chloe's father was fully as tall as his twin sons, his grip just as firm. But despite the words of welcome, the quick friendliness Luke had sensed in Daniel and his brothers was missing here. Clayton Caldwell looked at him as if he'd been measured and had come up wanting. "We've been waiting to meet Chloe's...friend."

Everything in Luke snapped to attention. Chloe's father, at least, couldn't be classified as "simple country folk." He wasn't accepting Chloe's supposed boyfriend at face value.

So this little charade might not be the piece of cake he'd been telling himself. The thought only made his competitive juices start to flow. When the challenges were the greatest, he played his best game.

Chloe had finally broken free of her mother and

sister, and he reached out to grasp her hand and draw her close against his side. For an instant she resisted, and he gave her a challenging smile. *This was your invention, Chloe, remember? Now you've got to take the consequences.*

She leaned against him, perhaps a little self-consciously.

Luke smiled at her father. "We're happy to be here. Aren't we, sweetheart?" He tightened his grasp into a hug, faintly surprised by how warm and sweet Chloe felt against him.

"Yes." Her voice sounded a bit breathless. "Happy."

"Well, so tell me all about him."

Chloe had started for the dining room with a large bowl of potato salad, when Miranda caught her by the waist and spun her into the pantry. She went with a sense of resignation. She couldn't have hoped to avoid Miranda's third degree much longer. They'd always shared everything.

Miranda's green eyes glowed with curiosity. "You've been awful closemouthed, sugar. Come on, 'fess up. Are you serious about him?"

The question twanged inside her, reverberating like a plucked string. She tried to shut the feeling away. She didn't want to lie to her sister. Probably she couldn't if she tried. Miranda knew her too well.

"Serious?" She tried to smile. "I don't know if

serious is the right word. It's complicated. He is my boss, after all.''

Miranda eyed her sternly. "Complicated. That means you do care about him, but you don't know if it's going to work, right?"

"How did you get so smart, little sis?" She tried to turn their perpetual rivalry over the eleven months between them to her advantage, hoping to distract Miranda.

Miranda shook her head, but not before Chloe had seen the quick sorrow in her eyes.

"I didn't get smart quick enough, remember?"

"Oh, honey, I'm sorry." Chloe plunked the bowl onto the linoleum-topped counter and put her arms around her sister. "I shouldn't have said that." She'd wanted to distract Miranda, not remind her of the man she'd loved and the marriage that had ended almost before it started.

"It's okay." Miranda's strong arms held her close for a moment. "I'm okay. Really." She answered the doubt she must have seen in Chloe's eyes. "I'm happy. After all, I have Sammy and the family."

But not the only man she'd ever love. The thought lay there between them, unexpressed.

"I just want you to be happy." Miranda squeezed her. "You be happy, sugar, okay?"

"I'll try." Chloe swallowed the lump in her throat. People said that Caldwell women were destined to love only one man. If true, that didn't bode well for either Miranda or her.

She tried to reject the thought. She didn't *love* Luke. She admired him. She admired his intelligence, his tenacity, his ambition. She'd been touched by his kindness to her, by the unexpected, intangible longing she sometimes surprised in his eyes, as if he yearned for something he couldn't have. But that wasn't love.

The thought lingered at the back of her mind all through dinner. She watched as Luke turned to answer some question Theo had asked. The chandelier's light put shadows under his cheekbones, showing the strong bone structure of his face, the determined jaw, the quick lift at the corner of his mouth when something amused him.

It also showed a certain tension in the way his hand gripped the fork. That sent a ripple of unease through her. Was he just nervous about this charade he'd embarked on? Or was something else going on—something she didn't know about?

As soon as the meal ended Luke gravitated to her side. Her heart gave a rebellious little flutter as she looked up at him. "Get enough to eat?"

"I don't know how your family stays so thin if they eat like that every night." Luke patted his flat stomach. "One more of those buttermilk biscuits, and you'd have to roll me away from the table."

"They don't sit in an office all day."

He grinned, and the unexpectedly relaxed expression fluttered her heart once more. "Touché. I'll have to remember that." He glanced around the large room. "But the inn doesn't seem to have any guests right now."

"This is Gran's birthday weekend. They don't take reservations this weekend, so the whole family can celebrate."

"They turn away paying customers?" He seemed to imagine an entire row of Dalton Resorts executives, all frowning at such folly.

"They put Gran first, that's all." The defensiveness in her tone surprised her. "The Dolphin Inn isn't a Dalton Resort."

"Obviously not." His lifted eyebrow spoke volumes. "Anyway, this isn't a busy time. We don't start getting a lot of guests until Easter weekend." It had never occurred to her to wonder why the inn wasn't more successful than it was. *We make enough to get by,* Daddy always said. She shouldn't have to defend her family's values, but that seemed to be what she was doing.

"I can understand why, if you close down for a birthday party."

She came perilously close to losing her temper with him. "If you—"

"Gran's here," Miranda called from the porch.

Every other thought flew from Chloe's mind, and she raced out the door. Gran marched up the shell path. Chloe met her halfway, to be wrapped in arms still as strong as ever. Gran's familiar lily-of-the-valley scent enveloped her.

"Gran, it's so good to see you." She pressed her cheek against her grandmother's.

Gran held her back a little, putting her palms on Chloe's cheeks. Her gaze was every bit as laser-like, in its way, as Luke's.

"'Bout time you were getting home, child. Where's this young man of yours?"

"I'm right here—"

She spun at the sound of Luke's voice, smooth as cream, behind her. He held out his hand to Gran.

"I'm Luke Hunter, Mrs. Caldwell."

Gran focused on him. Every one of Chloe's nerve endings stood at attention. How had she ever thought she'd get away with this? Why had she let Luke maneuver her into it? Gran's wise old eyes saw everything. They'd see through this.

But Luke seemed to be standing up well to that fierce inspection. After a moment, he asked, "Will I do?"

"Guess it'll take a bit of time to decide that." Gran looked him up and down. "You look a little fitter than I figured, for a city fellow."

"So do you. I expected someone a lot more frail."

He shot a challenging glance toward Chloe, and she felt herself shrivel. If he told Gran what she'd said, she'd never live it down.

"Chloe must be fibbing about the number of candles on your cake."

Gran gave a little snort that might have been a chuckle, and then nodded shortly. "Might as well

call me 'Gran.' Everyone else does.'' She took
Luke's arm. "Let's go set on the porch a spell.''

Chloe, following them, discovered she could
breathe again. But she couldn't fool herself that
happy state would last for long. She should never
have let Luke talk her into this. She just should have
told them all the truth and found some way to live
with the disappointment in their eyes.

Gran settled in her favorite rocker. The others filtered out of the house to receive Gran's kiss and find
a place to sit. Nothing they had to do was so pressing
that they couldn't enjoy the warm spring evening.

Chloe perched on the rail, and little Sammy
hopped up to lean against her. Gran motioned Luke
to the seat next to hers, and Chloe felt as if she were
waiting for disaster to strike. Surely, sooner or later,
Luke would falter, and someone would realize he
was playing a part.

But Luke seemed content to lean back in his
rocker, his gaze moving from one member of her
family to another, letting them do the talking. What
did he think of them? It shouldn't matter to her, but
it did. And what did they think of him?

She took a breath, inhaling the sweet scent of the
azalea bushes around the porch. It mingled with the
salty scent of the water. *Home.* If she'd been plopped
here blindfolded, she'd know in an instant where she
was, just by the smell.

She glanced around at the familiar faces, and love
welled in her heart. She wanted to tell them the truth.

She didn't want to hurt Gran. She didn't want them to be disappointed in her.

Please, God. She wasn't sure what to say. *Please. I don't want to hurt them. Please just let me get away without hurting them.*

She probably should be praying for the courage to tell the truth and be done with it, but somehow she couldn't. In a long line of brave Caldwell women, she must be the one exception.

Sammy wiggled against her. "Gran, tell the Chloe story, please?"

Her breath caught. That was one story she'd rather Luke didn't hear, especially now. "Sammy, you must have heard that story a hundred times, at least."

He grinned up at her. Sammy's heart-shaped face came straight from Miranda, but those dark eyes of his were just like his father's, and just as apt to break hearts.

"But I love that story, Aunt Chloe. Don't you?"

"'Course she does," Gran said. "She's that Chloe's namesake, isn't she?" She glanced around.

Daniel groaned. "Have a heart, Gran. Sammy might just have heard it a hundred times, but I've heard it a thousand."

"Won't hurt you to listen again," she said tartly. "You might learn something." She turned her chair so that it faced Luke's. "Chloe's beau ought to hear it, anyway."

Chloe sent a helpless glance toward Luke.

He leaned forward, smiling at her grandmother. "I'd love to."

"Well, it's this way." Gran half closed her eyes, as if she saw the story unrolling in her mind. "Years and years ago, before there was a Caldwell Cove, a girl lived here on the island. Her name was Chloe. A wild creature, she was. Folks said she talked to the gulls and swam with the dolphins."

Sammy slid off the railing and went to lean against Gran's knee. "Wasn't she afraid?"

"Not she. She wasn't afraid of anything."

Completely unlike the modern-day Chloe. The thought inserted itself in Chloe's mind and clung like a barnacle.

"One night there was a storm. Not an ordinary storm, no. This was the mother and father of all storms. It swept ships from their courses and snapped the tallest pines like matchsticks. In that storm a boat capsized, throwing its crew into the sea. Only one sailor made it through the night, clinging to a piece of wreckage, all alone."

Gran's voice had taken on the singsong tone of the island storyteller. As often as they'd all heard the story, still everyone leaned forward, listening as intently as if it were the first time.

"What happened to him?" Sammy's voice was hushed.

"He was played out. Poor man could see the island ahead of him, glistening like gold in the dawn light, but he knew he'd never make it. He gasped a last prayer. Then, before he could sink, creatures appeared next to him in the waves, holding him up. Chloe and her dolphins. They saved him. They pulled and pushed him through the surf until he staggered up onto the sand and collapsed, exhausted. But alive.''

As often as Gran told the story, it never altered by an iota. She told it the way her mother had told it to her, and her mother before that.

Sammy leaned close. ''Tell what happened to them, Gran.''

Gran stroked his cheek, ''You know that part of the story— He opened his eyes, took one look at her and knew he'd love her forever. He was the first Caldwell on the island, and he married her and started a family, and we've been here ever since.''

''And the dolphin.''

''He carved for her a dolphin out of a piece of cypress washed up by the storm. They put it in the little wedding chapel, and folks said every couple who married under the gaze of the dolphin would have a blessed union. And so they have.''

Chloe's throat was so tight she couldn't possibly speak. It was plain silly, to be so moved by an old story that probably didn't have much truth left in it. But she was. They all were, even Luke. She could read it in his intent gaze.

''Is the dolphin still there? I'd like to see it.''

Luke must be aware of the strained quality of the

silence that met his question. Here was the ending to the story no one wanted to tell.

"Chloe's dolphin is gone," Gran said softly. "Stolen one night by someone—no one knows who." Her wrinkled hand cupped Sammy's cheek. "But the story still lives."

Chloe's father stood, the chair rocking behind him. With a muttered excuse, he walked inside, favoring his bad leg as he did when he was tired.

His departure was a signal. David stood, stretched and held out his hand to Sammy. "Come on, guy. Time you were in bed."

"But—"

He swept Sammy along, stilling his protest. "Best get some sleep. I need you to help me take Chloe and Luke dolphin watching tomorrow, okay?"

Gran smiled. "Seems to me Chloe and Luke could stand a bit of time away from family." Her hands fluttered in a shooing motion. "Go on, now. Take your gal out for a walk in the moonlight."

Fortunately, it had gotten dark enough that no one would be able to see her flush. "Gran, we don't need to take a walk."

But Luke had already risen and was holding out his hand to her. "Come on, Chloe. Do what your grandmother says."

Apparently she didn't have a choice. She stood, evading his hand, and started down the three steps to the walk. But by the time she reached the bottom, his hand had closed over hers. It was warm and firm, and the pressure of his fingers told her that if she tried to pull away, he wouldn't let her.

Shells crunched underfoot, then boards echoed as they walked onto the dock. Moonlight traced a silvery sheen on the water. The mainland was a dark shadow on the horizon, pierced by pinpoints of light. They came to a stop at the end of the dock and leaned on the railing.

Chloe cleared her throat. This was amazingly hard. "I'm sorry about that. Gran has certain expectations about what she'd call 'courting couples.' I should have warned you."

He turned toward her. She couldn't be sure of his expression in the soft darkness, but she thought he was amused.

"It doesn't matter, Chloe. She's right, this is a beautiful moonlit night. I don't mind taking a walk with you to fulfill her expectations."

It was the kind of phrase he'd use in reference to a business deal, and the language didn't mesh with the gentle murmur of waves against the dock and the cry of a night heron. He didn't fit here, and maybe she didn't, either, any longer. The thought made her shiver.

"You're cold."

Luke ran his hands down her arms, warming them, sending a thousand conflicting messages along her skin and straight to her heart.

"We should go in." But she didn't want to. She wanted to stay here with him.

"That would disappoint your gran." His voice teased. "I'm sure she'd expect me to warm you up in a more old-fashioned way."

Before she could guess his intent, he'd leaned forward. His lips touched hers.

The dock seemed suspended in space, and she put her hand on Luke's shoulder to steady herself. This was crazy. She hadn't bargained on this. The shape of his mouth felt firm against hers.

Crazy. This whole charade was crazy, but at this moment she never wanted it to end. Tenderness and longing swept through her in equal measure with despair.

Chapter Three

Luke frowned at his laptop the next morning. Chloe's face kept appearing on the computer screen, overlaying the words—soft and vulnerable, with the moonlight turning her skin to ivory.

He was trying to get down his impressions of the Caldwell Island area in a preliminary report. He'd settled in one of the rockers on the porch after breakfast, letting the herd of Caldwells scatter to whatever occupied them. He had to work, not think about Chloe.

That kiss last night had been a mistake. He'd begun by teasing her, but he'd let himself be carried away by the charade. The next moment he was kissing her, and he'd known in an instant he shouldn't have. You didn't get involved with people who worked for you. Chloe was too valuable to him as an employee to risk ruining that.

He had to concentrate on the job he'd come here to do. That was his ticket to success. His initial impressions of the island were favorable, but plenty remained to be determined. He'd focus on collecting the data he needed, not on how unexpectedly beautiful Chloe had looked in the moonlight.

"Hey."

He glanced up, startled to find Chloe next to him, and snapped the laptop shut. He'd have to tell her what he had in mind at some point, but not yet. Chloe, in denim shorts and a T-shirt, looked ready for anything but business.

"Hey, yourself." He'd already noticed that everyone he met here used that word as a greeting.

She glanced pointedly at the laptop. "Are you ready to go? We have a date with David and Sammy to go dolphin watching, remember?"

Dolphin watching, as in…taking a boat out. The huge breakfast Chloe's mother had forced on him turned to lead in his stomach. Or maybe it was the grits, gluing everything together. "Why don't you go without me? I have some work I'd like to get done."

"Work?" She frowned at the computer. "I thought you were taking the weekend off. What are you working on?"

He didn't intend to answer that question. "Just keeping up with some reports. I don't care much for boats."

Being on the water gives me the shakes. No, he

wouldn't admit that to her. He didn't like admitting it to himself. His childhood hadn't included a place like this, and there hadn't been swimming pools in the back alleys that had been his playground.

"Come on." She held out her hand. "The *Spyhop* runs as smooth as silk. Besides, it's the best way to see the whole area."

That was the only argument that would get him on a boat. She was offering him the chance to see just what he needed to, in an unobtrusive way. And he couldn't keep refusing without having Chloe guess that what he really felt was something a lot stronger than reluctance.

"Okay. I'll put the computer away and be right with you."

Fifteen minutes later he stood on the dock with Chloe, wishing he'd stuck to his refusal. "Kind of small, isn't it?"

"The *Spyhop?* She's a twenty-six-foot catamaran. You should see the crowd they fit on her later in the summer, when the visitors are here. I'm sorry she's riding so low, but the channel's tidal. It's not hard to get into the boat."

Chloe stepped from the dock down to a bench seat in the boat, then to the deck, balancing as lightly as if on a stairway instead of a rocking deck. She looked up at him.

"Need a hand?"

Aware of David and Sammy watching from the

boat's cockpit, he shook his head, grasped the post to which the boat was tied and clambered down. Okay, he could do this. Nobody needed to know that his stomach was tied in more knots than the mooring line. With luck, they wouldn't find any dolphins, making the trip short and uneventful.

David turned the ignition, and the motor roared to life. He waved at Chloe. "Cast off, will you, sugar?" He grinned. "Or don't you remember how?"

Chloe stuck out her tongue at him, then climbed nimbly over the boat's railing to perch on the narrow space at the back and lean across to untie the ropes. Luke had to clench his fists to keep from grabbing her. Chloe had probably done this all her life. She wouldn't thank him for making a big deal of it.

Then the boat started to move, and he clutched the seat and concentrated on not making a fool of himself. Chloe dropped onto the bench next to him and gave him an enquiring look. More to distract himself than because he cared, he nodded to the cockpit.

"I thought Daniel was the one who ran the tours."

"They both do, but David's the real expert on the dolphins. His degree is in oceanography, and he's officially in charge of the dolphin watch for this region."

"Degree?" He couldn't help the surprise in his voice. "But I thought—" What had he thought? That they were a bunch of uneducated hicks?

The amusement in Chloe's gaze said she knew just how surprised he was.

"David knows his stuff, but he doesn't really like doing the narrative for a boatload of tourists. Daniel does that." She smiled. "You know how it is in a big family. We each have our roles."

"I was an only child." At least, he guessed he'd been. Nobody had stayed around long enough to tell him. "Tell me about it."

"Well, Daniel's the oldest, so he always thinks he has to be the boss—"

She wrinkled her nose, something he'd never seen her do in the office. It intrigued him.

"David's the quiet twin. Miranda is the beautiful one. And Theo, whether he likes it or not, is always going to be the baby."

He found himself wanting to say that she was just as beautiful as Miranda, and quickly censored that. "And what about Chloe? What is she?"

He thought a faint flush touched her cheeks, but it might have been the sun. "Oh, I guess I've always been the tomboy. Having two older brothers does that to you."

He nodded toward Sammy and spoke under the rumble of the motor. "Where does Sammy fit in?"

She stiffened, as if he implied something with the question.

"Miranda was married briefly when she was eighteen. It didn't work out."

Her tone told him further questions weren't welcome. "Sammy seems to have plenty of family looking out for him." He recognized, with surprise, a twinge of jealousy. He hadn't had a father, either, but no one had stepped up to take on responsibility, at least not until he met Reverend Tom and his Fresh Start Mission.

"Yes." The tension in Chloe relaxed. "What with the twins, my father, my uncle, the cousins—he probably has more male role models than most kids."

"Lucky boy," he said, and meant it. The tempo of the motor changed suddenly, and he grasped the seat. "Is something wrong?"

Chloe looked surprised, then shook her head. "We're just going around the end of the island, into Dolphin Sound. There are a few of the summer houses I told you about, and that's the yacht club." She pointed to a covey of glistening white boats, lined up neatly along a dock. "Summer sailors," she said, as if dismissing them.

Waves slapped against the hull, and a fine spray of water blew in his face. He nearly ducked, but saw Chloe lift her face, smiling.

"Now you can see it." She leaned forward, sweeping her arm in a broad gesture. "This is Dolphin Sound, between Caldwell Island and the out-islands. Beyond is the ocean."

Luke drew in a breath. He might not be much of

a sailor, but he knew what would draw vacationers to a resort area. Sunlight sparkled on the sound and reflected from the white wings of seagulls. Small islands shimmered on the horizon like Bali Hai, with empty golden beaches and drifts of palmettos.

"It's beautiful."

"Cat Island, Bayard Island. Angel Isle." Her voice softened as she gestured to the most distant of the three. "My favorite."

Sammy scampered back to them, moving nimbly as the boat danced through the water. He touched Chloe's arm, then pointed. "Look, Aunt Chloe. They're here."

He followed the direction of the boy's hand, seeing only the gentle swell of the waves. "I don't—"

A silver crescent broke through the surface of the water, not more than twenty feet from them, describing a glittering arc as the dolphin plunged back beneath the waves. Before he'd caught his breath he saw another, then another.

"Chloe, get the camera," David shouted. "The whole pod is here."

Chloe yanked a camera from its case and knelt on the bench seat, snapping as one glistening shape after another wheeled before them. David throttled back, and the boat slowed to a stop, rocking gently.

"Oh, you beauties," Chloe breathed, leaning out perilously far.

He couldn't help himself—he had to grab the loop

on her denim shorts. "Be careful, or you'll be swimming with them, like your namesake."

She glanced back at him, face alight with laughter. "Can't do that. It's against the law to swim with wild dolphins now, much as I'd like to."

David left the wheel to grab a clipboard and jot down notes, murmuring as he did so. "One of the best sightings I've had lately. You two brought us luck."

"Look, Uncle David, that's Onion for sure." Sammy bounced next to Chloe on the seat. "It is, I know it!"

"Got it in one, Sammy. You're a good dolphin watcher." David reached out to tousle the boy's dark hair. "Your name will go in the log."

"You're really keeping track of them?" Luke glanced at David's notes, which certainly seemed to be some sort of official report. "Is this your job?"

"Job?" His glasses shielded David's brown eyes, but Luke couldn't miss the passion in them. "Not in the sense of being paid for it, that's for sure. We're part of the dolphin watch that runs all the way up the coast."

One of the dolphins balanced on its tail, looking at Luke with enquiring eyes and that perpetual dolphin smile. Luke stared back. "I'd think there would be money in this one way or another."

David shrugged, not seeming to care. "We make a bit on the dolphin cruises. That's enough."

Enough? Luke opened his mouth to argue, then closed it again. It wasn't his business to talk David into seeing what he had here. If he tried, he'd only emphasize the difference in their values. That would make staying any longer more difficult.

And he had to stay. He'd seen enough today to convince him of that. This place was the perfect site for the next Dalton Resort hotel, and setting that in motion would take more than a brief weekend that was already half over. His mind ticked away with all he had to do. Chloe could—

"She's always been able to do that," David said softly.

Luke turned. Chloe leaned over the railing, reaching out toward the dolphin, and the creature lifted from the water as if saying something to her. The curve of her body matched the curve of the dolphin, and the sunlight made both of them glow with a kind of harmony that startled and disturbed him.

It was as if the Chloe he knew back in the office had transmuted into a different being here, one as alive and natural and free as that first Chloe. He didn't know how he felt about that—but he did know it was going to make their relationship different in ways he couldn't even imagine.

"Chloe Elizabeth, I hear you brought a young man home for your family to meet." Her father's second cousin, Phoebe, squinted across the crowded dining room at Luke. "'Bout time you were settling down. When is the wedding? Not June, I hope. That's nowhere near enough time for your momma to get ready."

Chloe nearly choked on a mouthful of shrimp toast. Was that what everyone was thinking? "We're not ready to set a date yet," she murmured.

Cousin Phoebe gave her a sharp glance. "That's not what your gran says. She's already planning the wedding quilt for you. Asked me to look out some fabric for her, so I said I would. You'd best decide on colors soon, heah?"

The shrimp turned to ashes in Chloe's mouth. Could this get any worse? If she denied it further than she already had, Cousin Phoebe would be rushing off to Gran with the story. Perhaps she could distract her.

"Cousin Phoebe, is that Aunt June's daughter over there?"

The sight of another relative she could interrogate always appealed to Phoebe. She veered off, replaced immediately by Gran herself.

"Gran, are you enjoying your party?" Chloe hugged her, feeling a rush of love at the soft, papery cheek next to hers. And feeling, too, a rush of guilt. She shouldn't be letting Gran and everyone else believe a relationship existed between her and Luke.

Gran patted her cheek. "It's a good party, Chloe girl. But the best part is that you're here, and you've

finally brought a nice young man home with you.''
Gran's eyes twinkled. "Even if I did have to invite
him myself.''

The "nice young man" seemed to be the topic of
the day with her elderly relatives. Chloe glanced
across the room. Luke stood by the window, deep in
conversation with her cousin Matt. Matt, a television
news reporter who'd come all the way from Egypt
for Gran's birthday, ought to be able to talk about
something Luke would understand. She recognized a
similarity in them and wondered if Luke would see
it—they were both driven, intense, competitive.

"I think he's having a good time." She couldn't
actually bring herself to say she was glad Gran had
gotten her into this fix. In fact, the truth pressed
against her lips, wanting to burst out. If she told Gran
all of it, Gran would understand, wouldn't she? Or
would she look at Chloe with disbelief that her
granddaughter had behaved this way?

Gran held Chloe's hand, her gaze fixed on Luke,
too. "Maybe one of my grandchildren will finally
find a lasting love. I'd started thinking the dolphin
ruined that for all of you.''

Chloe blinked. "What are you talking about?''

A faint flush mounted Gran's cheeks. "'Spose
you'll think it nonsense.''

"You know I'd never think that. But what do you
mean? What dolphin?''

"Chloe's dolphin, child. What else?'' Gran's eyes

brightened with tears. "That dolphin carving disappeared from the church, and no Caldwell has been married under it since. It's not right."

"Gran, you're not superstitious, are you?" She'd known Gran mourned the loss of the dolphin that was part of the family heritage, but hadn't imagined it meant more than that to her. "You don't really believe that old story!"

Gran looked at her sternly. "Chloe Elizabeth, there are more true things in stories than you can explain. I'm not saying folks can't have happy marriages even though the dolphin's not there anymore. Look at your daddy and momma—they're as much in love as ever. But it seems to me God's plan got messed up when that dolphin disappeared, and we need to see him back where he belongs."

Gran had always had a strong streak of the romantic in her, but Chloe hadn't expected this. She didn't know what to say.

"Don't worry about it, Gran. We'll all find the right someone to love, eventually." It was the most comforting thing she could think of, though none of the grandchildren had managed a happy ending yet.

"It's not just that." The lines in Gran's face deepened as she looked from Chloe's father, on one side of the room, to his brother, as far away as he could get and still be in the same room.

The breach between her daddy and Uncle Jefferson had existed long before Chloe was born, an established fact all her life. Everybody on the island knew that Uncle Jeff called Daddy a straitlaced prig and a failure, and that Daddy felt his brother's ambition had killed off his honor. They kept up a semblance of civility for Gran's sake, but their feud obviously still hurt her.

"I'm sorry," she said softly.

"Not much we can do about them, I'm afraid. But as for you young ones—seems to me you've found someone to love, dolphin or no, haven't you."

"I don't know. It's not…not really serious between us—not yet, anyway."

Gran's wise old eyes studied Chloe. "Don't think you can fool me, Chloe Elizabeth."

Her heart stopped. "What do you mean?"

"I mean, I can see how well the two of you fit together. You care about him, don't you?"

She couldn't lie about it with Gran looking at her. "Maybe so. But that doesn't mean it's going to be a lifetime love or anything."

Gran patted her hand. "You just keep in mind that verse I gave you on the day you were baptized. God has plans for you, plans to give you hope and a future. You trust in that, you hear?"

She blinked back tears, thinking of the needlepoint sampler Gran had made—the one that went everywhere with her. "I'll try."

"Besides, now that Luke's here, maybe we can help things along."

Panic ripped through her. "Don't you dare do any matchmaking. If things are meant to happen between us, they will."

"No harm in helping it along. I want to see another Caldwell bride before I'm too old to enjoy it."

"Gran—"

"Are you ladies having a private conversation, or can anyone join in?"

Chloe's breath caught at the sound of Luke's voice. She'd been so intent that she hadn't noticed him cross the room to them. She looked up, trying to smile, hoping Gran hadn't heard that betraying little gasp. Hoping even more that Luke hadn't heard it. There were no two ways about it—the sooner they got back to Chicago and their normal lives, the better for everyone.

"Always glad to have a good-looking man to talk to." Gran fluttered her eyelashes at him outrageously. "Especially one that I haven't known since he was in diapers."

"Gran," Chloe murmured. *Just a few more hours, and we'll be on a plane. I'll forget this weekend ever happened.*

Luke's baritone chuckle was like a feather, tickling her skin. "If you want someone to flirt with, Mrs. Caldwell, I'm your man."

"Thought I told you to call me 'Gran'. Everyone else does. How are you liking Caldwell Cove, now that you've been here a spell?"

"Beautiful," he said promptly. "Now I know why Chloe is always talking about this place." He put his arm around Chloe's waist, and she tried not to pull away. "It's the most peaceful spot I've seen in years."

"Well, then, you ought to stay a bit longer." Naturally Gran would pounce on that. "Spring's a perfect time for a vacation. Why don't you two stay on?"

Chloe waited confidently for Luke's excuses— they had to get back to the office, he had other plans, anything. They didn't come.

"You know, that might not be such a bad idea." He squeezed Chloe. "What do you think, Chloe? How about if we take a few vacation days and stay for a while?"

If the rag rug at her feet had jumped up and bitten her, she couldn't have been more shocked. "Are you...?" *Crazy* was what she wanted to say, but she bit back the word. "I don't think you've thought this through. We have work waiting for us at the office." She flashed him a look that should have singed, but he just smiled.

"Work will always wait." He turned to her grandmother. "Don't you agree, Gran?"

Before Gran could answer, Chloe took a step away, her fingers biting into his arm. "Let's go out on the porch, *dear*." She added the endearment through clenched teeth. "I need to talk with you."

Fuming, she tugged him through the crowd, emerging at last onto the porch and a quiet corner. She swung to face him, anger overcoming the deference she usually felt toward him. "What on earth was that all about? Why did you let my grandmother think we might stay longer?"

"Because we're going to." His smile was the one he wore when he crossed swords with a business opponent. "You should know I wouldn't kid about something like that."

The porch floor rocked under her feet like the *Spyhop* in a storm. "I don't understand. We're leaving in a little over an hour. We have tickets for tonight."

"We can change those easily enough."

"Probably, but why should we?" Her head began to throb. "This charade was meant to last a brief weekend, remember?"

"Relax, Chloe." He leaned against the porch railing, but his face was anything but relaxed. "I'm talking business, not romance."

From the house she could hear the cheerful buzz of voices, of people having a good time and forgetting everything else in their celebration. But here, the sagging old porch had taken on the air of a corporate office.

"What do you mean? What business?"

His gaze seemed to grasp her. "Hotel business.

I'm looking into siting the next Dalton Resort hotel here, on or near Caldwell Island.''

"Here?'' She could only gape at him. "I don't understand.'' Then she did, and it hit her like a blow. "That's why you wanted to come here with me, isn't it. You wanted to check it out.''

You didn't come to help me. Disappointment filled her heart. She'd thought he had done this out of misguided kindness, out of that urge he had to direct everything, because he cared about her. He hadn't. He'd done it to advance his career.

He shrugged. "You needed to be bailed out with your family. I needed a good excuse for being here, so I could see if the area was suitable. It is. Now we have to stay until I can decide on a specific site and put the acquisition in motion.'' His gaze sharpened. "What's the matter? I thought you'd be jumping with joy at the idea of bringing a little prosperity to the old hometown.''

"It means change,'' she said slowly, trying to sort out her feelings.

"Of course, it means change. Jobs, for one thing. You're not going to tell me this area couldn't use a nice fat payroll.''

"I suppose it could.'' No more lean times when the fish didn't run. No need for young people to leave home to make a living. He was right, she should be happy.

In the room behind them, someone, probably her

father, had begun playing the fiddle. "Lorena," one of her grandmother's favorites. The haunting air stirred misty echoes of a past that wasn't forgotten here. It was an odd counterpoint to the discussion they were having. "I'd like to tell my father about this."

"Absolutely not." His voice snapped, and her gaze jerked up to his.

He glanced beyond her, toward the door, then clasped her arm and drew her to the end of the porch. He stopped there, his back to the house, his arm around her. Anyone looking out would think they were seeing a romantic tryst.

"Sorry." His voice lowered. "It's not that I don't trust your family, but you know what it will be like if word gets out as to why I'm here. Every landowner in three counties will be trying to con me into paying top dollar for a piece of worthless swamp. We can't risk it."

His arm was warm and strong around her waist. That warmth crept through her, weakening her will to resist. *We,* he'd said. They were a team, like always. "But...you can't mean to continue this charade even longer." She hoped she didn't sound as horrified as she felt.

"Why not?" He hugged her a little closer, and his breath touched her cheek. "We've been doing a good job so far. There's no reason for anyone to guess we're not involved."

"I don't want to tell any more lies to my family."
She tried to pull free, but he held her firmly.

"You don't have to lie. We just let things go on
the way they are." His voice was low, persuasive.
"Think about how happy they're going to be with
the results, if everything goes the way I think it will.
Good times come to Caldwell Island, everyone's
happy, we go back to Chicago. In a month or so, you
can tell your family we decided to date other people.
It's going to be fine."

No, it wasn't going to be fine, not at all. If she did
this, she'd have to spend another week, maybe
longer, pretending to be in love with Luke. At this
precise moment, with the revelation of his motives
still stinging, she didn't even like him very much.
But she was getting entirely too used to the feel of
his arm around her.

No matter how this worked out, one thing was
crystal clear. Chloe Caldwell was in deeper trouble
than she'd ever imagined.

Chapter Four

Luke shifted his weight restlessly, waiting for Chloe's response. He could feel her tension against his arm. It was as if everything in her resisted him. He wanted her cooperation—needed it, in fact. Didn't she understand that?

It was probably the first time he'd seen his competent assistant show anger toward him, and it startled and fascinated him. He'd always found Chloe a bit too controlled. Apparently when it came to her family, she could be passionate.

He bit back the urge to demand. He wasn't at corporate headquarters now. This was Chloe's turf, not his, and she was a different person here.

"Well, Chloe?" He tried to keep his voice gentle, as if he really wanted her input on the decision. It was tough to do, when the vice-presidency shimmered as close as the blossom from a trailing vine that brushed Chloe's hair and perfumed the air.

"I wish there were some other way of doing this." Her face tilted toward his, troubled.

He tamped down annoyance. "There isn't. And this is your future, too. Wouldn't you like to be secretary to a vice-president? You'll move along with me. I can't do without my right arm."

It was an argument that would have swayed him, but it didn't seem to have much effect on Chloe. If anything, the resistance strengthened in her.

"I don't like the idea of fooling my family."

He bit back the reminder that she was the one who'd started it. "This isn't going to hurt them."

"How can you say that? How would you feel if it were your family?"

Her question hit him right between the eyes. *My family, Chloe? What family? The father I never knew or the mother who walked away when I was six? Or maybe you mean the string of foster families who didn't want to keep me.*

He took a breath, locking those questions behind the closed door in his mind. He didn't let them out because they made him think too much of where he'd been instead of where he was going. He wouldn't let Chloe and her old-fashioned family make him start remembering.

"If it were my family," he said evenly, "I'd think about how much they'd benefit in the long run. They will, you know. There'll be more business for all of them once a resort hotel comes in. You know that as well as I do.''

She nodded slowly, her face still troubled. ''I suppose I—''

''Hey, cousin.''

Chloe turned, her face lighting with pleasure. She pulled away from him to hug the man who approached, abandoning their conversation in an instant. ''Matt. I haven't had a chance to talk with you yet. How are you?''

Luke leaned back against the porch rail, searching for patience, as Chloe and her cousin caught up with each other. This one was Matthew Caldwell— Chloe's grandmother had introduced them earlier.

Chloe turned back to him, her arm still around Matt's waist. There was no stiffness in her as she leaned against her cousin. Apparently her guardedness was only for Luke.

''I'm sorry, Luke, I'm forgetting my manners—'' The turn of phrase was an echo of her family's speech. Chloe's cultivated urban tones were dropping away, and she probably didn't even realize it.

''You've met my cousin, Matt Caldwell, haven't you?''

Luke nodded. Matt had the strength and height that marked all the Caldwell men, but his dark eyes looked as if they'd seen too much, and there was a somber cut to his mouth when he wasn't actively smiling at Chloe.

"We already talked about Matt's reports from the Middle East. A tough spot to be in right now."

Matt nodded. "And Gran's told me all about your new beau, Chloe Elizabeth."

Most of it imaginary, unfortunately. The thought startled him. Unfortunate that he wasn't Chloe's beau? No, of course it wasn't. Chloe was the last woman in the world he'd become involved with, for more reasons than he could count.

"So how long are you staying home this time?" Chloe's tone was teasing. "Long enough to satisfy Gran?"

Matt shook his head. "I have to head back right away. And you should know nothing short of settling down in Caldwell Cove for life would satisfy Gran."

"Good idea. Maybe if you were here, Gran would stop teasing me to come back. You could become the publisher of the *Caldwell Cove Gazette*."

"You know, some day I might just do that. But not today." Matt tugged gently at a lock of Chloe's hair. "How soon are the two of you leaving?"

Luke caught a sudden, almost anguished look from Chloe. Then she smiled, and he thought he must have imagined it.

"We're going to hang around for a while," she said as easily as if they hadn't just been arguing about it. "Luke's decided to take some vacation time."

"That'll make the family happy. Well, I'd better get back to the second cousins. I haven't given

Phoebe a chance to interrogate me yet." Matt held out his hand to Luke, hugged Chloe again and turned away.

The screen door banged behind Matt, and Chloe turned to Luke, straightening as if she faced something unpleasant.

"I guess that means we're staying." He watched her, wondering what she was really thinking.

"I guess it does." She shrugged. "I don't seem to have much choice, do I."

"You always have a choice, Chloe. I think you've made the right one." He reached out to brush a strand of hair from her face. His fingers touched her cheek, and the warmth and softness of her skin seemed to radiate up his arm.

He had a choice, too. If he were smart, he'd choose not to touch her again, not to take too much pleasure out of playing the role of her boyfriend. He suddenly realized the smart choice might be a difficult one to make where Chloe was concerned, and that surprised and disturbed him.

"Chloe, love, don't forget to water these in." Chloe's mother put a flat of marigolds into the trunk of the car the next morning.

"I'll take care of it." Chloe hovered, impatiently holding the trunk lid, ready to snap it down. She wanted to get moving before Luke came out and volunteered to go with her.

But Sallie Caldwell lingered, her strong, capable

hands brushing the flowers and releasing their spicy aroma. "Have you talked to Theo since you've been home?"

The question caught Chloe off guard. "Well, of course I've talked..." She frowned. Theo had been elusive yesterday. "I guess not much. Why? Is something wrong?"

Her mother looked up, and the sunlight gilded her cheeks and brought out the warmth and welcome in her golden-brown eyes. Chloe felt a fervent hope that she'd be as lovely when she reached that age. Her mother never seemed to age, even after five children.

"I don't know." She shook her head. "Theo's always been such an open child. All of a sudden he seems to be keeping secrets. Something's troubling the boy, and I don't know what."

"Adolescence, maybe." She remembered how she'd been at sixteen—full of dreams and impatient to get on with grown-up life.

"Maybe it is just that. But he might confide in you. Will you see what you can find out?"

"I'll try."

Her mother's smile broke through. "Well, I know you'll give him good advice, whatever it is." She touched Chloe's cheek lightly. "It's good to have you home."

Her mother was talking to her like another adult, instead of a daughter. It felt odd but gratifying.

"I'll try to catch him alone and see what's up."

She shifted her hand on the trunk lid. "I probably ought to get going. Gran will be waiting."

Nodding, her mother stepped away, and Chloe closed the trunk. She jingled the keys in her hand. "I'll see you later."

"Where are you going?"

Chloe jumped at Luke's voice, the keys slipping through her fingers. He made a lunge and caught them, tossing them lightly in the air and catching them again. He lifted his eyebrows as if to repeat the question.

She'd thought he was safely lingering over his coffee and one of her mother's famous sticky buns. Looked as if she'd been wrong. "I'm taking my grandmother to the cemetery." She hoped her tone was final enough that he'd get the message. She didn't want company.

He opened the car door, smiling. "Fine. Let's go."

"I really don't need any help." She could feel her mother's gaze on her as she reached for the keys. "I thought you had some work you wanted to do."

His fingers closed around the keys. "Nothing that's more important than this." He gestured to the car as if inviting her into a coach. "I'd love to see your grandmother again."

"Well, of course Luke wants to go with you." Her mother beamed at the man she no doubt envisioned as a future son-in-law.

She was outmaneuvered, and she could hardly

make a fuss in front of her mother. "Fine." She got into the car, trying not to flounce. "I'm ready."

Luke closed her door, said goodbye to her mother and slid behind the wheel. She inhaled the scent of his aftershave as he leaned forward to put the key in the ignition, and she clasped her hands in her lap. This was going to be a long morning, after a longer night.

She'd tossed and turned for most of it, trying not to wake Miranda, who'd slept serenely in the other twin bed in the room they'd shared most of their lives. She hadn't been able to erase the memory of those moments on the porch. She'd continued to feel Luke's strong shoulder as he pulled her against him, continued to hear his voice as he called her his "right arm."

Right arm. Not what a woman wanted to hear, but it was an accurate description of how he felt about her—and she'd better remember it.

"Directions?" Luke stopped at Caldwell Cove's single traffic light and looked at enquiringly.

"Sorry." She felt her cheeks grow warm and was glad he couldn't read her thoughts. "Just go straight along the water. See the church steeple? Gran's house is next to the church."

"Tell me something, Chloe."

"What?"

"Why didn't you want me to come with you this morning?"

So much for her belief that he couldn't read her

thoughts. She seemed to be transparent where Luke was concerned. "I just...it's hard to keep up this charade with Gran. I've never kept secrets from her."

"Never?"

She glanced at him, sure he was mocking her, but found only curiosity in his eyes. "Well, hardly ever. A lot of times it's easier to talk to a grandparent than a parent about things. You know how it is."

"No." He bit off the word, then shrugged. "I don't remember my grandparents."

"I'm sorry. I can't imagine life without Gran. She's a strong woman. One of a long line." She seemed to see all those Caldwell women, looking disapprovingly at the current bearer of the name. Maybe, if she'd been able to be alone with Gran today, she could have told her the truth.

"This house?"

When she nodded, Luke pulled to a stop by the gate in the white picket fence. She got out quickly before he could come around to open the door, then joined him on the walk. "Gran has a green thumb, as you can see." She pushed the gate open, and they walked up a brick path between the lush growth of rosebushes. "Hers is one of the oldest houses on the island."

The white-frame cottage was like Gran—strong, functional, enduring. Before they reached the black door, Gran opened it, seeming to accept Luke's presence as routine. She handed him a galvanized bucket filled with seedlings.

"Mind you put that someplace shady. I don't want those petunias wilting before we get them in the ground."

"Yes, ma'am." Luke smiled and held out his arm, as if he spent every day escorting an elderly woman wearing a chintz dress and a battered man's straw hat. "We'll take good care of them. And of you."

Chloe fell in behind as they started down the walk, foreboding growing. Luke being charming was something to behold, and her grandmother, flirting outrageously from under the brim of the straw hat, was even worse.

Please, Lord, just let me get through this morning. The verse Gran had given her popped into her mind and wouldn't be dislodged. If God did have plans for her future, she suspected those plans didn't include Luke Hunter.

"And that's Chloe's great-great-great-aunt Isabelle." Gran pointed to the worn headstone. "She kept her family fed and safe right through the war, and that was no small thing."

Chloe wondered if Luke realized Gran was talking about the War between the States, and then she decided it didn't matter. He was being polite and acting interested in Gran's litany of family graves, and that was the important thing.

"Your family's been here a long time."

There was a note in Luke's voice that she didn't recognize, and she wondered what it meant.

"Back to the first settlers," Gran said with satisfaction. "Caldwells belong here."

Chloe stirred restlessly. "Some of us have found lives elsewhere, Gran. Maybe we don't belong here any longer." *Did she?* That thought had been in her head too often since she'd been back.

Gran patted her hand. "You belong, all right. Your roots run too deep here to forget, even if you do run off to outlandish places."

"Matt will be safe." She knew her grandmother was thinking of Matt's early morning flight. "We'll hear from him again soon."

Gran nodded, then fanned herself with her hat. "Chloe Elizabeth, I'm going to set a spell on the bench. You finish, all right?"

"We'll take care of it, Gran. You relax."

"Are you sure she's all right?" Luke frowned, watching as Gran tottered off to settle on the wrought-iron bench under a live oak. "Maybe we should take her home."

"She's not tired." Chloe knew her gran too well to be fooled. "She's matchmaking. Giving us a chance to be alone."

She waited for a sarcastic response, but it didn't come.

Instead Luke gestured toward the gray stones, tilting across the long grass. "You do this often?"

"What?"

"Come here, plant flowers. Read off the names."

He obviously didn't understand the Southern attitude toward cemeteries, and she wasn't sure she could explain it in a way that would make sense to him.

"Gran would say it's a shame to the living if the family graves aren't taken care of properly. I've been doing this since I was a little girl. We all have. It feels natural to me." She touched a worn stone, and it was cool beneath her fingers. "This was the first Chloe."

Luke knelt, frowning at the faded words. "What's that beneath the dates? I can't make it out."

"Her Bible verse. 'May God grant you His mighty and glorious strength.' All of us have our own verses." She shrugged, a little embarrassed. "It's a family tradition—a scripture promise to live by. Gran gave each of us a verse on our baptism, just as her grandmother did."

He stood, and he was very close to her. "What's your verse, Chloe?"

She looked up at him, wanting to turn the question away with a light comment. His blue eyes seemed to darken, staring into hers with such intensity that she couldn't escape, and he took both her hands in his. Her breath caught in her throat.

"It's from Jeremiah." She forced the words out, trying to sound natural. "'For I know the plans I have for you,' says the Lord. 'Plans to prosper you and not to harm you. Plans to give you hope and a future.'"

"Hope and a future," he repeated softly. "That's a nice promise, Chloe Elizabeth."

The lump in her throat was too big to swallow, and she could only nod. It had been a mistake to bring Luke Hunter here. She should have known that it would be. Things had changed between them. They'd never be the same again.

But they'd also never be the way she sometimes wished they would be. Somehow, she had to accept that.

He had to stop letting these people affect him so much. Luke drove toward the inn after dropping off Chloe's grandmother, trying to dismiss the feelings that had crept over him in the cemetery. Trying to tell himself the whole thing was maudlin, or quaint, or silly.

It didn't seem to work. He glanced sideways at Chloe. She wasn't really that different here than she was in Chicago, was she? Maybe not outwardly, but inwardly... He felt as if he'd opened an ordinary-looking package and discovered something rich and mysterious.

He couldn't erase the sense that she'd introduced him to a new world, a world where family meant something other than a collection of strangers held together by law. Those moments in the cemetery had moved him in a way he'd never experienced, and he didn't know what to do with those feelings.

He'd like to categorize this whole visit as an expedition into the sticks. It could be an amusing story—something to entertain his acquaintances at the next cocktail party or gallery opening. He tried to picture himself talking about Chloe's family and their quaint customs. He knew instinctively that he never would.

Okay, he'd accept that. But he'd also accept the fact that none of this fit into his real life—not Chloe, not her family. He didn't understand them, and they'd certainly never understand what he came from. He had to get things back to business, and he definitely had to trample the insidious longing to share more of himself with Chloe.

"Looks as if your father's just coming in." He drew up opposite the dock and watched Chloe's father jockey his boat into position.

Chloe was out of the car before he could go around and open her door. "Come on. We'll give him a hand."

She jogged onto the dock, and he followed reluctantly. The water was higher than it had been the last time—meaning the tide was coming in, he supposed. Waves slapped against the wooden boards, making them vibrate uneasily beneath his feet. The salt air assaulted his nostrils, and the expanse of sky made him feel vulnerable and exposed.

He didn't have to like it here. He just had to look

at it through a businessman's eyes, so he could make the right deal.

"Hey, Daddy." Chloe grasped one of the dock supports and leaned out to take the line her father held, then made it fast. "Any luck this morning?"

"Nothing running." Clayton Caldwell cut the engine. "If we depended on my fishing to put food on the table, our bellies would be bumping our backbones—"

He glanced at Luke, and Luke read reserve in those clear eyes. Clayton hadn't decided what to make of him yet.

"Hop down and secure that aft line, Luke."

The small boat bounced, bumping against the dock, and Luke's stomach bounced with it. Hop down? He didn't think so. But saying no would declare him either a rotten guest or a wimp, and he didn't like either of those alternatives. Steeling himself, he took a step forward.

Chloe nipped in front of him and stepped nimbly down into the boat. "I'll get it, Daddy." She grabbed the line and looped it around the upright. "Have to show you I haven't forgotten how."

"I didn't think that, Chloe-girl." Clayton stepped easily up to the dock, then leaned down and pulled Chloe up next to him.

The man must be close to sixty, but his muscles seemed as hard as those of any bodybuilder. Clayton's level gaze rested on him, and Luke discovered he felt smaller under that calm stare. He didn't like it.

Chloe hugged her father, pressing her face against the older man's white T-shirt. "You've been saying the same thing about the fishing ever since I can remember. We haven't gone hungry yet."

Her father squeezed her, then released her. "Must be about lunchtime. You two coming?"

"We'll be along in a minute." Chloe leaned against the railing as if the dock's movement was as common as the ascent of an elevator. She waited until her father was halfway up the crushed shell walk, then turned to him.

"Are you all right?"

"Of course I'm all right." He didn't sound authoritative, just irritable. But he didn't care for the way Chloe looked at him—as if he needed her pity. "Let's go."

Chloe caught his arm, and her fingers were cool on sun-warmed skin. "You're afraid of the water, aren't you?"

"What makes you say that?" He gave her a look designed to prevent any further questions.

She smiled. "Well, it might be the way you gripped the seat when we were out with David and Sammy. Or the way you turned white when my daddy asked you to hop down on the boat. Don't you know how to swim?"

"Everyone knows how to swim." He'd forced himself to learn in college, when he'd realized that ability was taken for granted by his classmates. "I've just never liked it, that's all. Let's go up to lunch."

Her fingers tightened. "I'm sorry. This is a bad place to be if you're afraid of the water."

"I'm not afraid," he snapped. It was none of Chloe's business, anyway. What right did she have to push him? Maybe she'd be the one telling stories about this trip to amuse her friends—how the big corporate executive was afraid of a little water.

She shrugged. "It's nothing to be ashamed of. I just thought since you're here, maybe you'd like to try and get over it."

He forced himself to look at her. He didn't see amusement in her eyes, just concern, maybe friendship. He grimaced. "Have you been taking psychology lessons in your spare time, Chloe?"

Her smile sparkled like sunlight on the waves. "No. But as long as we have to stay for a week…"

She let that sentence trail off, but the challenge in her gaze reminded him that he was pushing her to do something she didn't want to do. It dared him to do the same.

"All right." He pushed away from the dock railing. "I guess you have a deal. Now can we go?"

She nodded demurely. "Of course." She led the way off the dock.

He should feel better once he was back on solid ground, following Chloe toward the porch. He should, but he didn't. Oh, it wasn't the business of getting over his fear. He could suck it up and pretend, if he had to.

What bothered him was considerably more personal. It was the realization that he'd just shown Chloe a piece of himself. It was a piece he always kept hidden, along with anything else that might make him vulnerable. He wasn't sure how Chloe had come far enough into his inner life to see it. Or how he'd ever get her out again.

Chapter[?]

goddess on land. He dried her off as well as he could,
it he could.

While it meant him some consideration, then she
could, during the cool coast and he'd just saved
Chloe a plenty, thought, it was a particular thing.
Her bedouin aloud which anything real ever made
more important. He gazed leisurely to her,
quarter course with at times life went and so very
very soon

Chapter Five

"**A**re you ready?" Chloe stood knee-deep in the shallows of the sound, steadying the kayak with her hand. The afternoon sun was hot on her shoulders. Later in the summer the water would reach the temperature of a warm bath, but now it felt pleasantly cool. They'd spent the past two days ostensibly sightseeing while Luke looked at possible hotel sites, but she'd finally gotten him to make good on his promise.

She watched Luke's face as he looked from her to the softly rocking two-person craft. He'd obviously clamped down hard on his feelings. This was the face he wore when he met a challenge in the business arena—impassive, determined, aggressive. If he felt any fear, he certainly didn't intend to show it to her.

"You're sure you know how to operate one of

these things?'' Luke raised straight black brows and prodded the kayak.

''Daniel and David had me out in one before I went to kindergarten.'' She braced it with both hands. ''Climb in and get the feel of it. We'll stay where we can stand up, I promise.''

And where no one would see them. She didn't say that out loud, but she knew it was in his thoughts. Luke would never want anyone to see him doing something he didn't do well. But she also knew that if he once started something, he wouldn't quit until he had mastered it.

He grasped the side of the kayak. ''Okay, Chloe. I'm going to trust you. But if you dunk me, I'll take it out of your salary.'' He climbed in gingerly, and she handed him a paddle.

''That might be worth it.'' Before he could react, she pulled herself easily onto the seat behind him.

Freed from the restraint of her grasp, the small craft curtseyed in the gentle swell. Luke grabbed the side, and she pretended not to notice.

''I'll paddle first.'' She dipped the paddle into the water, sending them forward. ''When you feel comfortable, join in.''

She stroked evenly and watched the tension in his shoulders. For a few minutes he didn't move. Then, slowly, he began to relax. He released his grip on the side and turned his head to glance back at her paddle. She saw him in profile—mouth set, eyes alert, finding his way in unfamiliar territory.

"I pull on the same side as you?" He dipped his paddle into the water.

"That's right, just not too deep. Don't worry about the rhythm. I'll match my stroke to yours."

The instant he started paddling, the kayak picked up speed. They skimmed across the water. His stroke, uncertain at first, settled into a rhythm, even though his hands grasped so hard that his knuckles were white.

"Not bad," he said. "Not bad at all."

"Just remember that you control the kayak. It responds to your movements. If you lean over too far, we'll both be in the drink."

He turned toward her enough that she could see his lips twitch. "As you said, it might be worth it."

She let him set the pace, her strokes compensating for his inexpert ones. Gradually his movements became smoother, and the grasp he had on the paddle eased. She could see the moment at which he began to enjoy it, and something that had been tight inside her eased.

She lifted her face to the breeze, pleasure flooding her. She'd told herself it was only fair that Luke do something he found difficult, given the situation he'd pushed her into. But she knew that wasn't the real reason she'd wanted to do this.

This was the world she loved. Maybe she didn't belong here any longer, in spite of what Gran said, but she did love it. Especially on a day like this, with sunlight sparkling on the water and the gentle murmur of waves kissing the shore. She watched droplets fall from the paddle, crystal in the light. She wanted Luke to love it, too.

No, not love it. That was too much to ask. But she didn't want to imagine him going back to Chicago and amusing his friends with stories of his stay here. She wanted him to appreciate her place and her people, no matter how alien they were to him.

She stopped paddling, reaching forward to touch his arm. His warm skin made her fingers tingle, and she tried to ignore the sensation. "Look."

He rested the paddle on his knees and followed the direction she pointed. She heard his breath catch as the dolphins broke the surface of the water.

"They look a lot bigger from this angle."

"We're at their level now." She smiled, watching the flashes of silver as the dolphins wheeled through the waves. "Sometimes they'll come right up to the kayak, as if they want to play."

"I think I'd just as soon watch them from a distance." Luke glanced back at her. "I'm sure you'd rather play with them."

"They're old friends." As she said the words, she realized how much she'd missed this. "They come back to the sound every year. Maybe..." She stopped, not sure she wanted to say it. It sounded foolish.

"Maybe what?"

She shrugged. "Sometimes I think they're the descendants of Chloe's dolphins."

He turned toward her, expression skeptical. "Isn't that a little fanciful?"

"I know it's not likely." She hated sounding defensive. Why shouldn't she believe that if she wanted to? "But the same pod does come back year after year. They belong here just as much as we do."

"Maybe you're right—"

His voice had softened, as if he realized it was important to her. As if he cared that it was important to her.

"But it looks as if they're done showing off for us today."

She nodded, watching the silver arcs disappear toward open ocean. "They're probably heading farther out to feed. And I don't suppose you want to go out after them...."

"I'll have to get a lot better before I want to chase down dolphins in this thing." Luke picked up his paddle. "But I'm willing to practice."

"Okay." She dipped into the water. "Let's head for the buoy. You'll be able to see that tract of land near the yacht club from there."

He nodded, adjusting his movement to hers, and in a second they were paddling in unison. Luke's stroke picked up speed, sending the kayak flying across the water.

"Are we racing?" she asked, meeting his speed.

He turned his head again to smile at her, and this time the pure enjoyment in his face set her nerves vibrating.

"Too bad we don't have anyone to race."

"Don't you mean anyone to beat?" she asked.

He shrugged. "That's the same thing, isn't it?"

Maybe to him, it was. His question resonated, disturbing her pleasure in the moment. Luke excelled in competition, and she'd gotten used to that over the past few years. It seemed natural back in their business world. Here his competitiveness struck a jarring note, reminding her of the differences between them.

"There's the yacht club—" She pointed. "Uncle Jeff owns the land that adjoins it."

Luke shaded his eyes. "Is it up for sale?"

"I'd guess anything Uncle Jeff owns is up for sale, if the price is right." She heard the censure in her words and regretted it. "Sorry. I shouldn't have said that."

"Why?"

Luke sent a puzzled look over his shoulder, and she realized he hadn't even reacted to the family problem that weighed on her. This was business. And theirs was a business relationship, nothing more.

"Never mind. Let's take a break." She shifted her weight, turning the craft toward shore. "We'd best put some more sunscreen on before we get burned."

They rode the waves to shore, then dragged the kayak onto the sand. Chloe dropped to the beach towel she'd spread out and dug in her bag for the bottle of sunscreen. She tossed it to Luke.

"So, what did you think?" She nodded toward the kayak. "Think you could get to like kayaking?"

"Not bad." Luke rubbed lotion vigorously on his neck and shoulders. "Not bad at all." He held out the bottle to her. "Thanks, Chloe. I'm glad you pushed me into it, even if you were just trying to pay me back."

She smoothed the lotion along her legs, watching the movement of her hand so she didn't have to look at him. "I can't imagine what you're talking about."

He grinned. "Chloe Elizabeth, your grandmother would be ashamed of you, telling such a big fib."

The tension she had been feeling slipped away in the warmth of his smile. She leaned back on her elbows, lifting her face to the sun, and closed her eyes. Couldn't she just enjoy the moment and forget about why they were here together?

"Tell me something, Chloe."

She opened her eyes. "What?"

Frown lines laced between Luke's brows. "Your father and his brother—what's going on there?"

No, it looked as if she couldn't just enjoy the moment. It was her own fault for mentioning Uncle Jeff. She might try telling Luke another one of her fairy tales, but she didn't think he'd believe it. She could tell him it wasn't his business—but she was the one who'd brought him here. Or she could tell him the truth and let him make of it whatever he wanted.

"My father and Uncle Jefferson don't speak to each other unless it's absolutely necessary." She hadn't realized how odd that sounded until she said it aloud to him. "I guess that seems strange to you." She sent him a defiant look.

He leaned on his elbow, the movement bringing him close enough that she felt the energy radiating from his skin.

"I'd say it was strange, yes. How long has this been going on?"

"Since I can remember." She swallowed, knowing that answer wasn't all of it. "Since they were teenagers."

He whistled softly. "That's a long time to live in the same small community with your brother and not speak. What happened?"

"They quarreled," she said shortly. She felt his gaze on her and knew she had to say the rest of it. "No one knows exactly why, but people guess over a girl. They seemed to go in opposite directions after that. My grandfather divided the family property between them. Daddy took the inn and Angel Isle. Uncle Jeff got the boatyard, the cannery and the real estate. He…well, my daddy would say he wheeled and dealed so much he forgot who he was. Forgot what it meant to live with honor." She shrugged. "And Uncle Jeff thinks my daddy is old-fashioned, self-righteous…" She stopped. What was Luke thinking?

"Must be hard on your grandmother."

He had hit on the sorest point. "Yes, it is. I wish I knew how to make it better, but I don't." She hated that helplessness.

He put his hand over hers. "I guess your family isn't so perfect, after all."

She sat up, yanking her hand away. "I never claimed it was." Her resentment spurted. "I suppose yours is."

"My family?" His mouth narrowed to a thin line. "No, Chloe, my family's not perfect, either. Not by a long shot."

A barrier had suddenly appeared between them. She couldn't see it but she knew it was there. All the sunlight seemed to have gone from the day.

Secrets. She'd always known Luke had secrets to hide—always guessed it had something to do with his family.

But he wasn't going to tell her, that much was clear. The illusion of friendship between them was just that—an illusion.

This was getting to be a habit. Luke sat on the porch late that afternoon, frowning at the computer screen. Once again, Chloe's face intervened, hurt evident in her eyes.

He hadn't meant to cause her pain with his questions earlier about her father. He'd just been curious, trying to figure out what made the sprawling Caldwell clan tick. But he should have realized he was prodding at a tender spot.

He glanced out at the water, absently watching a white sailboat curve across to the mainland. He hadn't imagined it would cause Chloe pain to talk about it. He had no basis for comparison when it came to families, happy or otherwise.

All the more reason he shouldn't get further entangled with Chloe and her family. He should let them get on with their work, while he got on with his.

He looked around, exasperated. The Caldwells were doing a fine job of that. Daniel and David had taken a few guests out on a dolphin cruise. Miranda had whisked out of the kitchen a few minutes earlier, deposited a pitcher of iced lemonade and a plate of molasses cookies at his elbow and disappeared again.

As for Chloe...he had to smile. Chloe was busy setting up a Web site for the inn. Her parents' reluctance had been almost comical, but she'd finally gotten through to them. It looked as if Chloe had absorbed a bit about marketing from Dalton Resorts.

He was the only one not getting on with his work. He wanted— He wasn't sure what he wanted, and that was an odd feeling.

Erasing the pain he'd seen in Chloe's eyes might restore his balance. Then they could go back to their usual businesslike relationship, with no more delving beneath the surface to discover unexpected facets of each other. That would be far safer.

Two figures sauntered down the lane. The smaller one stooped to pick up a shell, then skimmed it out across the water. Sammy and Theo, obviously home from school. They turned, saw him, and seemed to hesitate, as if his presence disturbed their usual routine.

The yellow pup raced around the house, throwing himself at Sammy in an exuberant greeting. The boy dropped his knapsack and tussled with the puppy, then boy and dog raced toward him, with Theo following at a more sedate pace.

"Hey." Sammy's gaze fell on the plate of cookies. "Molasses. Bet my momma made those. She always makes them for guests." He was obviously too polite to ask for one, but his eyes spoke for him.

"You're right about that." Luke slid the plate toward the boy. "I'm plenty full, but I don't want to hurt your mother's feelings by not eating these. You could do me a favor by taking some."

Sammy nodded solemnly. "I guess that would be okay." He took a handful of cookies, then smiled. "Thank you, sir." Clutching the cookies, he whistled to the dog and then charged inside, the wooden screen door banging behind him.

Theo mounted the porch steps and leaned against the rail. "Sammy always acts like he hasn't had a cookie in a week, but I happen to know Miranda put three in his lunch bag."

Luke tried to picture a childhood in this place, where someone put homemade cookies in your lunch bag and you came home to the same welcome every day. He was watching it, but he couldn't quite believe in it. People didn't live like this anymore, did they?

Apparently the Caldwells did.

He expected Theo to hurry off, as Sammy had, but instead he lingered. Something self-conscious in the boy's manner made Luke look more closely at Chloe's little brother.

Theo had the height of his brothers, but his weight hadn't caught up yet. He had the sun-bleached hair, too, falling on his forehead, and his father's hazel eyes. But where the older man's gaze was confident and unhurried, Theo had the eyes of a dreamer. A certain vulnerable something about his mouth reminded Luke of Chloe.

The silence stretched uncomfortably long between them. "So, how's school?" A stupid thing to say, probably, but he didn't seem to have any common ground with the boy.

Theo shrugged. "Okay, I guess, sir. Pretty boring, most of the time."

"I remember that." He'd usually found ways of livening things up that probably would never occur to Theo, and Chloe certainly wouldn't thank him for bringing them up. "What do you do after school? Any sports?"

"Not this time of year." The boy shifted uneasily against the railing. "Actually, I was thinking about getting an after-school job."

Luke was faintly surprised at that. "I thought they kept you pretty busy around here." Certainly the rest of the Caldwells seemed occupied with the family business.

"Guess they do." A flush touched the boy's high cheekbones. "A person wants to do something without his family once in a while. Didn't you?"

He hadn't had a choice in the matter. "I guess so. What's this 'something' you have in mind?"

Theo looked at his scuffed sneakers. "There's a job down at the yacht club. They're pretty busy just now with lots of colleges having spring break. I could work there."

Luke pictured the glistening white boats he'd seen moored at the yacht club, imagining the kind of people who owned them. "Sounds like a smart idea to me. That's the kind of place where you meet people who count."

"People who count for what?" Chloe asked.

He hadn't heard Chloe come out, but she stood a couple of feet from him. She was close enough that he could feel the anger, close enough to see the sparks. Obviously he'd made a tactical error.

"Theo and I were just talking." He heard the apologetic note in his own voice and wondered where it had come from. He didn't owe Chloe an apology for taking an interest in her kid brother, did he?

Theo slid away from the rail. "Guess I'd best see if Miranda needs any help." He vanished into the inn, leaving Luke to face the accusation in Chloe's eyes.

"You were encouraging him to take a job at the yacht club." She shot the words at him.

He closed the laptop and leaned back in the rocker,

meeting her gaze with his own challenge. "I'm not sure *encouraging* is the right word. We were talking about it. Don't you want me to talk to your brother, Chloe?"

"You implied that the yacht club people were important for him to know."

He stood, setting the chair rocking behind him, and put the laptop on the table. It looked incongruous next to the lemonade and molasses cookies, reminding him that he didn't belong here.

"I told him what I thought." He frowned at her. "Unless being back here has softened your brain, you know how important it is to know the right people."

She flushed, the color painting cheeks that were already glowing with sunlight. "That's what it's like in the outside world."

"What if Theo wants to live in the 'outside world'? *You* did. Are you saying he can't make the choices you made?"

She took a step toward him, her hands curling into fists.

"Theo is too young to make choices like that. And you certainly don't have the right to advise him."

"He came to me, Chloe. And you brought me here."

"Do you think I've forgotten that?" She glanced toward the inn, then lowered her voice. "This deception was your idea, not mine. You decided on it for business reasons, not because you wanted to do me a favor.''

''Maybe that's true.'' He wasn't going to let her get away with shifting all the responsibility onto him. ''But you're the one who created the situation in the first place, remember?''

''I know.'' She stood very straight, fists clenched. ''But that doesn't mean it's all right for you to interfere with my family. I don't want you giving Theo advice. I don't want his values to be—''

''Contaminated by mine?'' Whatever fascination he'd felt in seeing Chloe stand up to him disappeared in a wave of anger. ''There's nothing wrong with my values. They're realistic in the world out there—'' He jerked his head toward the mainland.

''Caldwell Cove is different.''

''Don't kid yourself, Chloe. This place may seem like Shangri-La, but sooner or later it will get dragged into the twenty-first century. Isn't that what you're trying to do with your Web site? Your brother might need the kind of values that lead to success.''

''I don't want Theo influenced by you.'' Chloe threw the words at him. ''If you can't accept that, then maybe you'd better leave right now.''

Chapter Six

Horror at what she'd just said flooded Chloe. Was being back on the island causing her to take leave of her senses? She couldn't talk to her boss that way.

Apparently Luke felt the same. His face tightened, and his ice-blue eyes chilled her to the bone. "Is that really what you want, Chloe?" His voice was deceptively soft, but she'd heard that deadly calm before, directed at other people. Her job hung in the balance.

"I'm sorry." The words came out in a rush. "I shouldn't have said that."

But it was true. The thought came out of nowhere. She tried to reject it but she couldn't. She didn't want Theo absorbing the values that seemed so natural to Luke.

Please, Lord. The prayer also seemed to come from nowhere. *I don't know what to do here. I don't know what I want, and I certainly don't know what's best.*

"You have a right to say what you believe." He shifted his weight so that he stood an inch closer to her. He was close enough that she could feel the iron control he held over his anger. "Is that what you believe, Chloe?"

"I don't..." She stopped, took a breath, started again. "I can't mix business and family together. Maybe that's one of the reasons I like working in Chicago. Having you here, letting my people believe we're involved—it's just too hard."

She expected a withering response. Instead she felt his ire seeping away as he considered what she'd said.

"All right." He nodded, still frowning. "I guess I can understand your feelings. The question is, what are we going to do about it?"

He actually seemed to be trying to understand. Maybe he'd been as surprised by their quarrel as she had. She could breathe again.

"If we told my parents the truth..."

"No."

His sharp response told her *that,* at least, hadn't changed. He tried to manage a smile, but it didn't have much humor in it.

"That's the one thing we can't do. I have too much of my time and reputation invested in this location now. If I don't come up with a proposal, I can kiss the vice-presidency goodbye."

The way his face hardened on the last words told her he wouldn't do that. It meant too much to him—maybe more than anything else in his life, certainly more than her old-fashioned values.

"All right."

She took a deep breath, trying to find an alternative they both could live with. She'd like to feel that the two of them were on the same team. She'd always felt that—until now.

"I guess I can understand that. But I'm not going to lie to anyone. And I don't want you to give Theo any more advice." Her mother's worries about the boy flitted through her mind. She'd said she would help, but this certainly wasn't what she'd intended.

"Agreed." He clasped her hand as if they'd just sealed a deal, and his fingers were strong around hers. Their warmth swept inexorably up her arm, headed straight for her heart.

She stepped back, breaking the connection. "All right, then." She reached behind her for the door, needing to escape. "We'll leave it at that."

"Just one thing—"

Luke's voice stopped her. She turned reluctantly to look at him.

"Maybe you ought to give a little thought to what you're saying to your brother, Chloe."

She looked at him blankly. "I don't know what you mean."

"You don't want him taking on my values. But

your life is an example more potent than whatever I
might say to him. Isn't it?''

Chloe tried to find an answer to that question
throughout another mostly sleepless night. She
couldn't remember when she'd felt so torn—between
Luke and her family, between the past and the future.
She'd made a promise to Luke, and she'd always
been taught that a promise had to be honored. Taught
by her daddy, to whom honor was everything.

The future, that was what worried her the most.
She turned over, trying to keep the bed from creaking
in protest, and stared at the ceiling. Would Daddy
say that if he knew what promise she was keeping?
Moonlight filtered through the curtains, sending de-
signs across the ceiling as the branches of the live
oak swayed. When she was a child, she'd imagined
whole stories taking place in those moving shadows—filled with castles and dragons and knights on
horseback.

Miranda's even breathing from the other bed was
oddly soothing. Miranda had made her choices, and
as difficult as they'd been, she never seemed to doubt
the road she was on. Chloe envied that certainty.

Where was this adventure going to end? She
couldn't picture it, couldn't believe that things could
ever go back the way they'd been between her and
Luke, between her and her family.

Maybe that was bound to happen sometime. She
could hardly expect to find happiness while working

for Luke—not when that meant holding her feelings
secret in her heart. As for her family—her relationship with them had changed, and she hadn't even
realized it. She'd looked for her career off the island,
thinking that was the only way to be her own person.
She'd been tired of being just one of the crowd of
Caldwells.

Now—she thought of her mother, talking to her
about Theo as if she were a friend. Of the pleasure
she'd found in being useful here. Of the way her
experiences with Dalton Resorts had begun to trans-
late to ideas for running the inn. Things changed,
whether she wanted them to or not.

She turned again, and her restless gaze fell on the
framed sampler with the words of her Bible verse
embroidered on it, which was propped on her bedside
table. She couldn't leave it behind in Chicago, so it
had come with her.

As the words reverberated in her mind, she felt her
tension begin to seep away. *Hope and a future.* She
might not be able to see how God's plans were going
to work out, but knowing they existed should be
comfort enough. Her body relaxed, her eyelids drift-
ing closed.

She'd meant what she said to Luke about not telling her family any lies. But as Chloe watched her
father talk with Luke over coffee in the breakfast
room the next morning, she wondered if she'd gone

far enough. Maybe she should have specified that
Luke not tell any lies, either.

"Excuse me, miss, could I have another pot of
tea? This one isn't hot enough."

Chloe managed a smile for the elderly guest whose
tea water was never hot enough. She didn't mind
being pressed into service at breakfast—she'd done
it since she was old enough to carry a tray. She *did*
mind not being able to hear what Luke and her father
were talking about.

Why? The question nagged at her while she
brought a fresh pot of tea for table four, replenished
the dish of homemade strawberry jam at table six and
whisked a nearly empty breakfast casserole dish from
the buffet table. Why did it bother her to see her
father with Luke?

Maybe it was her fear that the two of them could
never see eye-to-eye on anything. Clayton Caldwell
lived by a few simple rules—rules he'd taught his
sons and daughters from the day they were born.
*Trust the Lord, and He will guide your ways…. Tell
the truth, even if it's painful…. A man's word is his
bond, and without it he has nothing.*

Her father wouldn't understand the kind of business world Luke operated in, though he'd probably
equate it with Uncle Jeff. Luke would never understand her father. He'd mistake her father's sense of
honor for naïveté, just as her father would mistake
Luke's sense of competition for dishonesty. No, it

would be far better if she could keep the two of them apart until this game had ended.

Carrying the carafe of coffee, she approached their table with a sense of determination. "Daddy, would you like a thermos of coffee to take with you?"

"I'm not going just yet, Chloe-girl." He held out his mug, his sharp eyes inspecting her. "Fact is, I'm not going fishing at all today. Your momma's been pestering me to take a picnic lunch, go over to Angel Isle, check out the cottage. I'm thinking we'll do that today."

Well, at least that would get him out of Luke's company for a while. "Sounds like a nice idea. Don't worry about anything here. I'll keep an eye on the desk."

Luke smiled and held out his mug for a refill. "Actually, your father invited us to go with them to the island."

Only long years of practice kept her from dribbling coffee onto the blue-checked tablecloth. "Don't you have some work you want to do?"

Luke was probably longing for her to give him an excuse to get out of it, she assured herself. He probably had no desire to go out on the boat again.

"Not at all," he assured her blandly. "Sounds like a great idea."

She set her lips into what she hoped resembled a smile. "Fine. I'll just go help my mother get things ready."

Trying to avoid her father's gaze, she whisked her-

self off to the kitchen. Daddy knew his children only
too well. He'd always been harder to fool than her
mother—not that she'd spent a lot of time trying to
fool either of them, even as a child. But she'd seen
the twins try, and fail, too many times. This cozy
little trip together was not a good idea.

And what had given Daddy the idea? He didn't
take the morning off just to— The thought struck her
with a certainty she couldn't deny.

Gran and her matchmaking.

She pressed her palms to overheated cheeks. She
could just imagine the conversation.

*All Chloe's young man needs is a little push to
propose,* Gran would say. *It's up to us to see he gets
it. Chloe will be the next Caldwell bride.*

Now what was she going to do about that?

She still didn't have an answer an hour later, when
she stood on the dock handing a picnic basket to
Luke. He'd already been on the boat with her father
when she'd come down. What had they been talking
about? She tried to think of one single thing they had
in common, and couldn't. Except, possibly, her.

She gave Luke a sharp look as she accepted the
hand he held out, and climbed onto the *Spyhop.* "Are
you sure you want to do this?" She spoke under the
noise of the motor. "Daddy would understand if we
begged off."

Luke looked at her questioningly. "Don't you trust
me around your father, Chloe?"

She definitely should have laid down the law to

Luke about her father, as she had about Theo. "It's not that." Since she didn't believe herself, she felt quite sure he didn't believe her, either. "I just thought this wouldn't be much fun for you. The water might be rougher out on the sound today."

"Then, I'll have to depend on you to keep me safe, won't I?"

His low voice teased her, and she felt a little ripple of…what? Longing for a relationship with him in which teasing spoke of affection? That was a dangerous way to think.

Luke turned away to help her mother on board, drawing her gaze. Had he borrowed the jeans and T-shirt from one of her brothers? It certainly wasn't his usual garb. Before this trip, she'd have said he wouldn't look at ease in anything but a business suit. But he seemed perfectly at ease now, with the T-shirt stretching across broad shoulders and looking even whiter against his tanned arms.

She shouldn't be noticing that, she told herself firmly, bending to stow the hamper in the locker and taking the jug of sweet tea her mother handed her. She should imagine Luke right back into one of his expensive suits. Maybe then she'd be able to get through this trip.

She started forward, but her mother caught her arm.

"I'll go up front with your daddy, honey." She nudged her toward Luke, smiling. "You sit back here and keep Luke company."

Matchmaking, she thought despairingly. *Oh, Gran.*

Before she could come up with a really good reason to sit forward, her father was asking Luke to cast off the lines. When she made a move to do it, Luke edged past her and leaned across to the dock.

"I've got it." He nodded toward the seat. "You sit down and be a lady of leisure this trip."

He must have watched her handle the lines the last time, because he did it perfectly, with not the slightest hesitation to show how much he disliked leaning out over the water. He even coiled the lines the way she had.

"Very nice," she murmured, when he sat down next to her. "You must have been taking lessons."

"Somebody talked me into it." He smiled, then draped his arm casually across her shoulders. "Don't forget, you have to hold on to me if I get nervous."

"Aren't you afraid I'll push you in, instead?" She wouldn't turn her head to look at him. His face was too close to hers, and she was already too aware of the weight of his arm against her.

He squeezed her shoulders. "Not a chance," he said softly in her ear. "I trust you, Chloe. You'd never let me down."

She tried not to respond to that, tried not to think that he meant anything by it. He trusted her as his assistant—that was all.

The *Spyhop* rounded the curve of the island, passing the yacht club dock. The sound stretched in front of them, waves glistening in the sunlight. A laughing gull, squawking, flew overhead, probably hoping they'd give him something for his lunch. On the horizon the islands beckoned, lush and mysterious.

She felt Luke's movement as he inhaled deeply, tilting his head back as if to take it all in.

"Beautiful," he murmured.

He turned toward her, so that she felt his breath against her cheek.

"It's really beautiful, Chloe. Thank you for bringing me here."

He hugged her, his cheek warm against hers as if they really were the couple her family believed them to be.

Chloe smelled like sunshine. Funny that he'd never noticed that before. Luke held her protectively, feeling her slim figure sway against him as her father sent the boat in a wide arc toward the island. He was enjoying this, maybe a little too much.

Enjoyment had been the last thing on his mind when her father had invited them to go along today. It had been on the tip of his tongue to say no, but Clayton Caldwell's shrewd gaze had suggested he wouldn't buy an easy excuse. And then Luke had thought of Chloe and the concerns she'd brought up the day before.

He'd been angry at first over her attitude toward his talk with her brother. After all, he hadn't approached Theo. Theo had come to him.

But he couldn't help being impressed by how

much she cared about her family. Her passionate defense of them was outside his experience, and he didn't really understand it. The only thing he had to compare was his friendship with Reverend Tom and the debt he owed to the man who'd taken him off the streets and given him a future.

Well, he was determined to try his best to fit in here, for Chloe's sake. This trip gave him an excuse to look over the area and make Chloe's parents happy. Unfortunately, Chloe didn't seem to be reacting quite the way he'd hoped. She sat stiffly within the circle of his arm, as if she'd pull away at the first excuse.

He squeezed her shoulder. "Come on, Chloe." He spoke softly under the noise of the motor. "Lighten up. You're not on your way to the guillotine."

That startled her into meeting his eyes. "I'm not acting as if I am."

"Sure you are." He moved his hand, brushing her hair. It flowed like silk over his fingers. "I know you don't like the pretense, but can't we at least be friends?"

Her mouth tightened, and her eyes were very bright. "Friends, or boss and assistant?"

"Friends," he said firmly.

"Maybe being friends isn't such a good idea. When we go back to Chicago..." She stopped, and her gaze eluded his. "Well, it might cause problems."

That unsettled him. He hadn't really considered

what their relationship was going to be like when they went back to the city, back to their relative positions in the company. He'd only thought about that corner office, with the vice-president title on the door.

"Don't be ridiculous." It came out more sharply than he intended. "We've always worked well together, and we always will. Nothing will change between us."

"Maybe," she said softly, looking away. "Maybe you're right."

Annoyance shot through him. All right, he hadn't thought through that part of it very well. So he couldn't go back to looking at Chloe as if she were nothing more than an efficient assistant. That wasn't necessarily a bad thing, but Chloe looked as if it were the end of the world.

He opened his mouth to tell her so, but the motor suddenly throttled back and their privacy vanished. Chloe slid to the edge of the seat, putting several inches between them.

"There it is—Angel Isle." She pointed.

"Looks pretty good, doesn't it, Chloe-girl?" Her father swung the boat toward a dock, cutting the motor so that they drifted in.

"Looks great to me." Chloe scrambled to fasten the lines. "Not a thing has changed."

"Well, that's how we like it." Her mother bustled back, pulling out the picnic hamper.

Luke got to his feet slowly. He should help her,

but for the moment he could only stare at the scene spread out in front of him.

The dock anchored one edge of a wide, shallow curve of shoreline. Palmettos and moss-draped live oaks fringed a pristine, untouched sandy beach. Waves rolled in gently, rippling onto the sand like a woman shaking a tablecloth. It was as isolated and exotic as a castaway's island.

Chloe had already scurried up onto the dock, and she held out her hand to him. Whatever reservation he'd sensed in her a moment ago was gone now. Her eyes sparkled with eagerness, almost golden in the sunlight.

"Hurry up. I want to see the cottage."

He climbed out and followed her off the dock and onto the shell-strewn path, leaving her parents behind on the boat. He could already see the house, although he wouldn't call it a cottage. The building was long and low and nearly as large as the inn. Gray-shingled, with a screened porch running the length of it, it fit into the setting as if it had grown there.

"Pretty big for a cottage, isn't it?" He caught up with Chloe and took her hand.

She looked startled but she didn't pull away. "I guess. I mean, the family has always called it that. Years ago, they used to summer here. That was in the days when everyone went to the outer islands in the hot weather. But that got too difficult once they opened the inn. Now we use it for shorter visits, family reunions, that sort of thing."

He tried to visualize Angel Isle as he'd seen it from the water. It had looked virtually deserted. "Are there any other houses?"

"Others?" She went up the porch steps. "No. Just ours."

He hardly wanted to look at the idea that was forming in his mind, for fear he'd see some flaw in it.

"I suppose all this is some sort of nature preserve or something, then?" That might explain why no one else had built here.

"No, of course not."

Chloe had already hurried across the porch. Standing on tiptoe, she pulled a key from a hook at the top of the door frame, then unlocked the door. She swung it open, and he had a quick glimpse of a spacious room dominated by a massive brick fireplace.

He was more interested in answers to his questions than he was in the Caldwell cottage. "Then, why hasn't anyone else built on Angel Isle?"

"Because it belongs to us. My daddy, I mean. I thought I explained that. Grandpa split things between Daddy and Uncle Jeff." Her face clouded. "Uncle Jeff thought Daddy a fool for taking Angel Isle, when the other property was so valuable."

That must be a piece of the feud between the brothers. "So all this belongs to your father."

She nodded, then went quickly across the room and began throwing open curtains and unhooking shutters. "You want to give me a hand?"

He followed her, mind busy, excitement building as he helped her tug on a recalcitrant shutter. He'd have to find out exactly how much land there was, but there should be some way of working a deal with her father. Because he'd just found the perfect place for the next Dalton Resort hotel.

He looked at Chloe, intent on the shutter. Did she really not know what he was thinking? He wanted to shout it to her, wanted her to share his excitement, wanted to feel her encouraging him to another success.

But that was Chloe back in their other world. Here—here he didn't know how Chloe would react if he told her. Would she be excited and happy?

For an instant he felt resentment. He wanted his old Chloe back, the faithful right hand who always anticipated his needs and backed him no matter what.

"There!" The shutter popped open and sunlight streamed into the room. It lit Chloe's skin, tangled in her hair, made her eyes shine. "Isn't that better?"

"Better," he echoed. Would it be better if he had his old Chloe back? Maybe so, but he wouldn't trade this Chloe for an instant.

Chapter Seven

What did this mean? Chloe tried not to stare at the expression on Luke's face, but she couldn't help it. He looked as if he were seeing something for the first time.

"Chloe." He said her name softly, holding out one hand toward her, palm up. Something seemed to stir in the shaft of sunlight from the window, as if the very air between them would speak.

Her breath caught. She took a step toward him, and the movement was as slow as wading through the surf. In an instant they would touch—

"How's everything look?" Her father's voice shattered the silence.

Chloe's face flooded with heat as she turned toward the door. Luke turned, too, moving away from her quickly. Was he relieved they'd been interrupted? Or maybe she'd just imagined the whole thing.

"Let me take that for you." Luke reached for the thermos her mother carried. "Can I bring anything else from the boat?"

"Not a thing." Her mother set the thermos on the table. "We're just fine." She exchanged a knowing look with Chloe's father. "You young people go on out and enjoy the day. We'll take care of things here."

"No. I mean, we'll help you." Chloe couldn't be sure, but she thought Luke's expression echoed her words.

"Nonsense." Her mother shooed them with her hands, for all the world like Gran. "Luke hasn't even seen Angel Isle yet. You show him around, honey. We'll straighten up in here, then we'll have lunch when you all get back."

They didn't seem to have much choice. Chloe headed for the door, hearing Luke's footsteps behind her. He probably regretted he'd gotten out of bed that morning.

She didn't look at him as she took the path back to the shore, but she could feel his presence as surely as if they touched. She didn't say anything. What could she say that wouldn't make this more awkward?

When they reached the stand of sea oats that marked the dunes, she heard him chuckle. The sound was a bit strained, but at least it meant he wasn't angry about her parents' machinations.

"Subtle, aren't they?" he said.

"Sorry about that." She tried for a lightness she didn't feel. "I'm afraid my grandmother recruited them to do a little matchmaking."

"I thought as much." He strode beside her on the hard-packed sand of the beach. "Don't worry about it, Chloe. If we can cope with a corporate near-takeover, we can cope with a little family match-making."

Her tension eased at his words, reminding her of the difficult days three years ago when Dalton Resorts's future hung in the balance. They'd all worked around the clock until the danger was over. Luke had put things back on a business basis, and that was clearly what he wanted. The moment when they'd stood looking at each other in a shaft of sunlight might never have been.

"Of course we can." That was best, she assured herself. "We're a team." That was what he'd always said, and she'd taken comfort in the sense that they were on the same side.

"Always. You're my right hand, remember?"

She nodded, matching her step to his long stride. She had to stop imagining anything was changing. She ought to be happy. That meant they'd be able to go back to normal, once this whole thing was over.

She took a deep breath, inhaling fresh salt air. She wasn't sure she knew what "normal" was any longer, or if it was something she wanted or could even live with.

Maybe she'd better concentrate on introducing this

place that she loved to Luke. If he could appreciate it the way she did, that would be enough for the day.

They rounded the heel of the tiny island, and the sea breeze lifted her hair and cooled her cheeks. "Now you see why they're called the out-islands." She pointed to the horizon. "There's nothing beyond them but ocean."

Luke shielded his eyes with one hand. "It's so clear I feel as if I can see all the way to Europe—" He turned, glancing back at the island, and she heard his quick intake of breath.

"What on earth is that?"

"Strange, isn't it." Chloe walked to the nearest uprooted pine, its trunk washed free of bark, its roots a tangled mass of bleached tendrils. She rested her hand on the massive trunk that had been scoured clean by the waves. "The power of the sea."

Luke stroked the smooth wood. "Do all these trees wash up here?" He looked down the beach, where tree after felled tree formed a bizarre landscape of twisted roots and gnarled limbs.

"Not washed up," she corrected. "They grew here, until the tide started coming in farther and knocked them down. None of the outer islands are stable on the seaward side—that's why the buildings face the sound. The ocean's taking a bite out of Angel Isle."

Luke put both palms on the trunk and hoisted himself. He reached down, smiling an invitation. She felt herself smile in response as he took her hand in a firm clasp, lifting her up to sit next to him.

She settled on the smooth surface, trying to ignore the warmth that radiated from Luke, trying not to look at how the sun glinted on his bare arms.

"It's beautiful," he said quietly, leaning back on his hands. "Weird, but beautiful, like another world."

She'd better concentrate on the scenery, too. "That's what I've always thought. Another world." She tilted her head back, letting the breeze ruffle her hair. A pair of brown pelicans swooped low over the water, and she envied their view. "Or maybe a little piece of heaven."

"I guess you could look at it that way."

His response was noncommittal, the careful answer he'd give a business colleague if the subject of religion came up. Suddenly she wanted to push him—she wanted more.

"I've always felt closer to God here than anywhere else." She didn't bother trying to edit her words or shield her beliefs from him. "And I've always thought God must love it, too, or He wouldn't have made it so beautiful."

For a moment she thought he'd ignore her. Then he frowned.

"That sounds like something an old friend of mine would say."

"An old friend?" Was she actually about to see into his private life?

"Reverend Tom—"

He was looking out at the pelicans, but she didn't think he saw them.

"A good friend."

"Was he your minister when you were a child?" He wouldn't answer; she knew that. He never talked about his childhood.

"You could say that, I guess." His mouth tightened to a thin, unrevealing line.

"You don't look as if the thought makes you very happy."

He shot her a look that gave nothing away. "It just reminded me that I haven't been in touch with him in a long time. That's all."

"Maybe you should be."

His face tensed, and she knew she'd gone too far.

"We don't fit into each other's lives anymore."

He said it as if that ended the matter. The friend was another secret Luke didn't intend to share. If they were in the office, she wouldn't have pushed this far. But they weren't in the office.

"Would he like this place?"

Luke shrugged. "He wouldn't appreciate the potential."

For a moment she could only stare at him. "What do you mean?"

His gesture took in the strange shapes of the drowned forest. "This. Hasn't it occurred to you what a commercial draw this could be? With the right kind of promotion, people would pay to visit this."

Disappointment was an acrid taste in Chloe's mouth. A commercial draw—that was all he could see. Maybe she'd been wrong about the depths she thought he hid. Maybe he was nothing more than the surface persona—the success-driven businessman who didn't care about anything but profit.

The thought shouldn't hurt her heart as much as it did.

"Look out!"

Luke took a quick step back, holding the kitchen door for Miranda the next morning as she darted through with a steaming pot of coffee. She flashed him a smile.

"Go on back. Chloe's in there."

He wasn't actually looking for Chloe, but there didn't seem any point in trying to tell Miranda that. He'd come down this morning with the single aim of talking to Clayton Caldwell about Angel Isle.

He helped himself to coffee from the sideboard while he scanned the dining room. The large oval table where they'd sat for dinner the first night was pressed into service as a breakfast buffet. Smaller tables for guests clustered around it and overflowed into the hall and onto the porch.

Only a few guests had come down this early. Chloe's father was usually one of the earliest people down, but the chair where he always sat was empty.

Luke frowned. After their return from Angel Isle, he'd spent the rest of the day learning everything on the public record about Angel Isle. Now he was keyed up and ready to roll, but his instincts told him to proceed cautiously.

Anyone could see that money was tight for this branch of the Caldwell clan. The inn couldn't be bringing in much, and Clayton Caldwell had a lot of people depending on him. He should be glad to sell part of Angel Isle for the price Dalton Resorts would be willing to pay.

But would he? Luke frowned, swirling the coffee with his spoon. He seemed to hear again Chloe's soft voice, her Southern accent more pronounced the longer they stayed here, talking about how much the place meant to her. He was used to dealing with people who had their eyes on the bottom line. Chloe's clan was something different, and he couldn't judge how they'd react to his proposal.

He'd handled difficult negotiations before. The key was simply to find the right approach. He'd sound out Chloe's father cautiously, and when he hit on the thing that would make the man sit up and take notice, he'd know it.

He set down his cup. Where was Clayton? Maybe Chloe knew. He headed for the kitchen.

The swinging door opened on a scene of controlled chaos. Sammy was taking silverware from the dishwasher, clattering it onto a tray, while Miranda cut fruit into a bowl, interrupting herself to stir some-

thing on the stove. Chloe slid a steaming casserole
from the oven. All of them were talking at once, and
the teakettle whistled noisily above the din.

Retreat seemed the obvious course, but that
wouldn't tell him where Chloe's father was.
"Chloe?"

She looked up, cheeks red from the oven's heat.
"Hand me that pot holder, will you, please? I'm
about to burn myself on this."

He snatched the pot holder she indicated from its
hook and slid it under the hot dish, helping her negotiate the course to the scrubbed pine table.

"Ouch." Chloe snatched her fingers away,
blowing on them. "Thanks." She flashed him a
smile.

"Anytime. Where…"

But Chloe had already turned to her sister. "Why
does Mom keep these worn-out pot holders? It's not
as if she doesn't have plenty of them. Gran makes
them faster than anyone can use them."

Miranda filled a pot with coffee. "You know
Mom. She hates to throw anything away."

"Chloe…" He tried again.

Before he could frame the question, Miranda had
put a coffeepot in his hand. "You wouldn't mind
taking that to the dining room, would you, Luke? Our
mother is taking one of the cousins to a doctor's
appointment in Savannah, and we're a bit short-
handed."

He caught Chloe's horrified look. Obviously it

never would have occurred to her to ask him to help. But that was because Chloe knew he was more accustomed to giving orders than taking them.

"Sure, no problem." He started for the door with the coffee. "I've always wanted to be a waiter."

Miranda's green eyes sparkled with amusement. "Busboy. You're just a busboy. You have to work your way up to waiter."

He smiled back at her and pushed through the swinging door. This busboy would take the coffee in once. Then he'd find out where Clayton Caldwell was and make his escape.

When he returned to the kitchen, Chloe had taken over the fruit bowl, and Miranda and Sammy had disappeared.

"Did your crew desert you?" He set an empty coffeepot in the sink.

Chloe sliced a kiwifruit with quick, even strokes, the colorful slices falling into a pattern across the top of the bowl. "Miranda had to get Sammy ready for school. I told her I could finish."

He reached for the steaming teakettle, and she gave him a startled look.

"What are you doing?"

He shrugged. "There's an elderly woman at the table by the window who says her tea water isn't hot enough. Guess I'd better take her a refill, or I might get demoted. What comes below busboy?"

"You don't need to do that."

Chloe picked up the glass fruit bowl, and he could tell she was trying to hide embarrassment.

"I'm sorry—I mean, Miranda shouldn't have assumed you'd want to help."

"What's the matter? Don't you think I can?"

Her color heightened. "It's not what you're used to."

"Believe me, Chloe, nothing about this place is what I'm used to." He had an unexpected stab of longing. If he'd had a childhood with this kind of family... "That doesn't mean I can't pitch in and help."

"Are you sure?" Her forehead wrinkled with doubt.

He should be looking for Clayton. Funny that all of a sudden helping Chloe seemed to supercede that.

"I'm sure," he said firmly. "You take the fruit. I'll get the tea water."

He followed Chloe into the dining room, watching as she deftly tidied the buffet table. She moved from table to table, smiling as she played the gracious hostess in her jeans and a red-checked apron. She'd undoubtedly forgotten about the dab of flour on her cheek. She was adorable.

"You're the fiancé from the big city, aren't you? Chloe's beau." It was the woman who'd asked for fresh tea water, and she held out her cup expectantly.

"We're not—" He stopped. He couldn't begin to explain his relationship with Chloe to himself, so he certainly couldn't to anyone else. "Yes, ma'am." He poured the tea water. "I'm Chloe's beau."

Chloe heard that. He could tell by the way she carefully avoided looking at him as she brushed by. That avoidance annoyed him, and for a moment he wondered at himself. It was nothing, he argued mentally. He was playing a role; that was all.

He caught up with Chloe at the kitchen door, aware of a number of pairs of eyes on them. *Might as well give them something to look at,* he decided with a flicker of rebellion. As the door swung, he dropped a kiss on Chloe's cheek. Her skin smelled like peaches. He didn't want to pull away.

She stepped back, startled and wary, once they were alone in the kitchen.

"What was that for?"

"We had an audience." He nodded toward the dining room. "I was just giving them what they expected."

Chloe's golden eyes darkened. "Don't bother."

She clattered a tray onto the counter, and he had the sense that she counted to ten. But when she turned back to him, she was smiling.

"I'll be fine now. I don't need any more help."

It shouldn't bother him to be dismissed that way. After all, he hadn't wanted to help in the first place. They'd drafted him.

"Fine. Do you know where your father is?"

"Out back, with Theo." She frowned. "Why?"

"Just something I wanted to ask him." He started

for the back door. He'd taken enough detours for one morning. It was time he got on with business.

Before he reached the door, it swung open. Theo charged through, barreling past Luke as if he didn't see him. The door slammed hard enough to rattle the glasses.

"Theo—" Chloe didn't get the rest of her sentence out before Theo's trajectory carried him on through the swinging door and out of the kitchen.

She looked at Luke. "What's going on with that boy?"

He would have said it looked like Theo had been having words with someone, but before he could, the door opened again. Chloe's father stalked in, limping a little, his face like a storm at sea. He looked past Luke, zeroing in on Chloe.

"Chloe, do you know anything about this notion of Theo's about working at the yacht club?"

Chloe wiped her hands on a tea towel, probably buying time. "He mentioned something about it the other day."

"You know how I feel about that. You should—" He stopped abruptly, seeming to realize he was about to say something he didn't want to say in front of Luke. "Don't know what's got into him," he muttered, and slammed back out the door.

In the silence that followed, Luke raised an eyebrow. "What was that all about?"

"Nothing," Chloe muttered, turning away from him.

He caught her wrists. "Come on, Chloe, give. What's going on between Theo and your father? Why is he so upset about the yacht club job?"

"My father just doesn't like the yacht club crowd." Her gaze clouded. "I don't really know all the reasons. He's had some bad experiences with people like that."

People like that. Wealthy people, socially prominent people. The kind of people who frequented a Dalton Resort hotel. This could be a complication.

Luke studied Chloe's averted face. She'd said she didn't know all the reasons. And it certainly didn't look as if she wanted to confide any to him.

"Seems kind of hard on Theo," he commented, wondering if that would draw her out.

That brought her troubled gaze up to meet his. "I know. I wish I'd gotten Theo to talk to me about it. Mom asked me to try and find out what was bothering him, and I didn't. I haven't been a very good big sister to him."

"Chloe, it's not your fault." His instinctive desire to comfort her surprised him. He lifted his hand to brush the flour from her cheek. "You've only been here a few days. Let's face it, we've been pretty busy dealing with your family's matchmaking."

She smiled, her smooth skin moving against his fingers. He cupped her cheek with his palm, a wave of tenderness sweeping over him at the warm, silken feel of it. Chloe's eyes widened, and he had the sense that neither of them had taken a breath in too long.

He took a cautious step back, drawing his hand away. Convincing Chloe's father to sell him the land on Angel Isle would be difficult. Convincing himself that there could be anything between him and Chloe would be insane.

He knew what he wanted his life to be like. He'd known since he was a cold, dirty kid, standing on the outside and looking at people who had it all. He'd known he was going to be one of them someday.

Sweet little Chloe Caldwell didn't fit into that world. He knew that. So why did it leave such a bad taste in his mouth?

Chapter Eight

"**W**hat are your plans for my life, Lord?"

Chloe didn't realize she'd asked the question aloud until she heard the words echoing in the otherwise silent chapel. She glanced around. No one was there to hear her wrestle with the question that had occupied her since those moments with Luke in the kitchen that morning.

She'd forgotten, during her years in Chicago, just how difficult it was to get two minutes alone to think when her family was around. She'd also forgotten how close to God she felt in the chapel, where generations of faith permeated the very air. Her church in Chicago had dynamic preaching, wonderful music, active programming. But somehow she'd never felt quite as attuned to the Lord there as she did here in a simple wooden chapel.

She leaned forward in the pew, pressing her palms against her eyes as if she could iron away the image of Luke's face. One moment he'd been touching her, caressing her cheek, his gaze filled with what she'd thought was caring. The next moment he'd moved away, face shuttered, closing her out. She felt as if the prize had been within her grasp and she'd stumbled, losing it.

What happened, Lord? Her feelings for Luke must have been written all over her face. He must have seen.

Maybe that was the answer. He'd seen, and he'd backed away. He didn't want to be involved with her.

She took a deep breath and leaned back, her hands dropping to her lap. If that was what he felt, she'd live with it. After all, that was what she'd been doing all these years. Only since they'd come to the island, since they'd embarked on this ridiculous venture, had she begun to hope for more.

The afternoon sun slanted through the old stained-glass windows, tinting her skin with rose and green where the light fell on her. She let her gaze move from window to window, drawing comfort from each—Jesus with the blind beggar, Jesus with the children, the Good Shepherd, and her own favorite, Jesus walking on the water. The glass waves reminded her of the sound, whipped by the wind. She took a deep breath, feeling the peace she'd longed for begin to seep into her.

Then she looked at the thing she'd been avoiding since she walked into the chapel—the empty shelf behind the pulpit where Chloe's dolphin had once stood. Strange, that the bare space seemed so wrong to her. She'd never even seen the dolphin. It had disappeared before she was born, but still she felt its loss.

Poor Gran. The chance of recovering it was about as slim as the chance that Chloe would find a happy ending with Luke.

She got up slowly, not sure she'd found an answer but comforted nonetheless. It was time she got back to the inn. Her Web site had gone up that morning, and she wanted to see if there'd been any response. And she had some advertising ideas she wanted to talk to her mother about. As long as she was here, she may as well put her resort expertise to good use.

She was pulling the church door closed behind her, when she heard his step on the walk, recognizing it as surely as if she saw him. She took a steadying breath and turned.

"Luke. What are you doing here?"

He gestured toward the rental car that was pulled up to the curb, and she realized he wore chinos with a short-sleeve dress shirt, his uniform on the rare casual day at the office.

"I'm going to Beaufort to take care of a few things. Do you want to go with me?"

Spend the next few hours alone with him, when

her feelings were rubbed raw? She didn't think so. "I'm not dressed for that."

He shook his head impatiently. "You look fine. Come with me. I want to talk to you."

His tone was the one he used at corporate headquarters, the one that carried the assumption of obedience. She wavered. If she went along, she could point out some other hotel site possibilities she'd been thinking about.

Then she saw her grandmother hurrying toward them from her house. "Gran?" She took a few steps to meet her. "Is something wrong?"

Gran grasped both her hands. "You're needed at home, Chloe Elizabeth. Theo has run off."

"Run off?" Business was banished from her mind. "Why?" Well, she knew the answer to that question, didn't she—the quarrel with Daddy. "What makes you think he's run away?"

"He wasn't in school today. Sammy came home without him. Some of his things are gone, and his boat is missing. Your mama's worried half to death. I think you'd best get looking for him."

Chloe turned to Luke. "Did you know about this?"

His face tightened as if she'd accused him of something. "I heard some of it. Your father didn't seem upset. He said Theo was old enough to look out for himself, and he'd come home when he was

ready.'' Luke shifted impatiently. "I have to get on
the road.''

Her gaze shifted from Luke to her grandmother.
They each looked back with the calm assurance that
she'd do what they wanted, which was impossible.

She realized suddenly that she was seeing with the
clarity she'd sought in the quiet chapel. Being back
on the island brought things into focus. She was
caught between wanting Luke's approval and wanting her family's respect. She certainly wasn't going
to have both, and if the truth came out about their
charade, she'd probably end up with neither.

But in this situation, at least, her choice was clear.
"I'll take the *Spyhop* out and look for him, Gran."
She kissed her grandmother's soft cheek. "Don't you
worry about a thing. I'll find him."

She didn't look at Luke, because she didn't want
to see the irritation she knew would be written on
his face.

Why on earth was he doing this? Luke cast off the
line, then grabbed the rail of the *Spyhop* and slid into
the seat nearest Chloe, as she eased the boat away
from the dock. He should be on his way to Beaufort
right now to fax documents to the legal department,
not setting off on a wild-goose chase.

"Are you sure you know how to do this?" Chloe
looked small and vulnerable behind the wheel.

She flashed him a smile. "I've been doing it since

I was big enough to hold the tiller.'' She jerked her head toward the locker. ''You might want to get a couple of slickers out, though. Those clouds look like they're working up to some rain.''

He made his way cautiously to the locker. He'd had it all figured out. He'd take Chloe along on the trip to the county seat, he'd tell her what he was doing and he'd parcel out some of the work to her. It would be exactly as if they were back in the office. That would get the situation back to normal between them. It would eliminate the possibility of any more moments like the one when he'd cupped her cheek in his hand and wanted to hold her forever.

Instead of taking the rational course, he'd given in to the expectation in her grandmother's face. Of course, Chloe's beau would go along with her to find Theo. Gran couldn't imagine anything else.

So he'd found himself agreeing, and he still didn't quite know why that was. He didn't ordinarily have trouble saying no in response to other people's expectations. Gran Caldwell would be a force to reckon with in the business world, if she decided to embark on a career.

He found two yellow slickers, pulled them out and moved cautiously back to Chloe. ''These okay?'' He had to shout over the roar of the motor.

''Fine.'' Chloe grabbed one of the slickers and struggled to put it on while holding the wheel. It flapped in the stiff breeze.

"Let me." He caught the sleeve, holding it while Chloe shoved her arm into it, then pulling it into place. He practically had his arms around her. He gritted his teeth. So much for that resolution.

"Thanks."

She turned the wheel expertly, sending them in a wide arc around the end of the island. Again he felt that sense of surprise at her competence.

Or did he mean admiration? He'd never pictured Chloe like this, but she was completely at home driving the speeding boat, the wind ruffling her hair and making her cheeks glow.

"Do you know where he's gone?" He braced himself with a hand on the rail as they made the turn toward the sound.

She nodded, frowning. "I think so. I hope so. Where we all tend to go when we're in trouble. Angel Isle."

"If that's the case, why are we going after him? Why not just let him come home on his own?"

He still didn't quite get this. When he was Theo's age, he'd already been virtually on his own for years. Nobody would have come looking for him if he disappeared, unless a foster parent decided to report him to the cops.

"Because my grandmother's worried. And my mother."

"And because you think you let Theo down."

Chloe frowned across the sound. "I guess."

He followed the direction of her gaze and frowned, too. No sunlight on sparkling waves today. Sullen gray water greeted him, and the wind whipped up whitecaps. A hazy mist hung between them and the islands. He pulled the slicker on.

"I suppose it won't do any good to tell you you're not responsible for him."

She shook her head. "He's my brother."

That obviously ended it, as far as Chloe was concerned. She accelerated, sending the boat rocketing across the waves, and his stomach lurched as each wave hit. Maybe the cold spray in his face would help keep him from getting sick. He held on and hoped.

An eternity later, Chloe eased back on the throttle. Luke peered toward the dock on Angel Isle. "I don't see his boat."

"Doesn't mean he's not here." Chloe pulled the *Spyhop* into position at the dock. "He might have beached his boat along the south end. That's what I did, when I ran away."

"You?" He swung the rope around the post, faintly surprised at how familiar the movement felt already. "I can't imagine you running away, Chloe."

She turned off the ignition. "I was about twelve. It's a terrible age—not quite anything. I thought Daniel and David had been picking on me, nobody was sympathetic, I was lost in the crowd—you know, usual twelve-year-old angst."

"So you ran away to the island." Chloe would never understand the reasons *he'd* had for running away. They'd had nothing to do with teasing big brothers. His stomach tightened. They'd been ugly reasons, some of them.

"I even packed a lunch." She climbed up to the dock. "I wonder if Theo thought of that." Her mouth tightened, as if she pictured Theo lost, cold, hungry.

He climbed up beside her. "What happened? Did you get tired of it and go home?" Maybe talking about that childhood adventure would keep her from obsessing about Theo.

"Not exactly." She stopped, pushing the hood of her slicker back as she looked up at him. "I told you I always felt close to God here. This was a good place to communicate with Him. By the time I'd tried to listen to what He wanted, I knew I had to go home."

She didn't seem to expect any comment to that. She just turned and walked quickly toward the cottage.

He followed, trying unsuccessfully not to think about her words. Had he ever had that kind of reliance on God's wishes, even when he was with Reverend Tom? He didn't think so. He'd always, even at the worst of times, known what he wanted for his life. He hadn't questioned those goals.

He didn't intend to start now.

Halfway to the cottage, the rain that had been

threatening arrived. Chloe jerked her hood up and bent into the wind. "Come on. Hurry."

He jogged after her, clutching the hood that the wind tried to rip from his head. This was no spring shower. The rain didn't come down in drops, it came in waves, as if someone were emptying buckets of it. The wind tore across the island, shrieking in his ears. It bent palmettos and whipped Spanish moss into a wild dance.

They pounded up the steps, and Chloe wrestled with the knob. In an instant they were inside. He slammed the door and could hardly believe the sudden silence with the storm locked outside.

"Nasty." He looked at the rain, pounding against the windows as if it wanted to break in.

Chloe shrugged out of her slicker. "Typical. It won't last too long, but we're stuck here until it eases up." She took a couple of steps into the room. "Theo? Theo, are you here?"

Nothing answered her but the clatter of rain and the howl of wind.

Luke hung their wet slickers on the pegs by the door. He looked around the large room so that he wouldn't look at Chloe, standing there with her hair tumbling in her face and a lost look in her eyes.

"This is nice," he said. He might have said home-like, except that he'd never known a home like this. He'd seen it the last time they came to the island, but he'd been so preoccupied with his idea that he'd barely noticed the surroundings.

A brick fireplace dominated one wall, and hooked rugs brightened the wide, weathered floorboards. Worn, overstuffed chairs and a couch seemed to invite him to sit. The bookcases under the windows overflowed with everything from children's books to a fat old encyclopedia.

"Yes, it is." Chloe's reply sounded absent.

She obviously still worried about her brother, and he was suddenly ashamed. He knew why he wanted to distract her. Not because it would make her feel better, but because it would make him feel better. He didn't want to deal with her emotions.

He crossed to her, reaching out to take both her hands in his. "Chloe, it'll be all right."

Her eyes were bright with unshed tears. "I just want to find him."

"I know." His fingers moved to caress her hands almost without his conscious intent. The pulse in her wrist beat against his skin. He wanted to tell her Theo would be fine, but he couldn't say anything. All he could do was look at her and long to hold her in his arms.

Chloe looked on this place as a sanctuary, but it was dangerous to him. It made him too aware of how he'd closed himself off to God. Of how he'd tried to close himself off to Chloe. Neither of those efforts was working.

* * *

Chloe's heart pounded somewhere in her throat, so that she couldn't speak if she wanted to. Not that she did. She just wanted to stand there with Luke's hands enclosing hers and watch the play of emotions in the deep blue of his eyes.

Luke released her hands as carefully as if they were made of glass. He took a step back and cleared his throat.

"Chilly in here. You mind if I start a fire?"

So that was it. She tried to swallow her disappointment. "I'll do it."

But he was already halfway to the fireplace. "I might be a city slicker, Chloe, but I know how to light a fire."

That left her nothing to do but try to forget what he'd made her feel. Or, more to the point, keep him from knowing what she felt.

Her throat tightened. She'd thought she could be content with the status quo, but that didn't work any longer. She knew now what she should have faced a long time ago. If he couldn't care for her, she couldn't go on working for him. She'd be better off making a clean break as soon as possible and getting on with her life.

The future Gran insisted God had for her might well be here. Maybe she'd had to go away to get the experience that would make her valuable to the family.

Flames licked upward from the crumpled paper

Luke had lit, quickly catching the dry pine needles from the basket on the hearth. The chill that had permeated the large room retreated.

She cleared her throat. "Would you like coffee? I can put some on."

"No." He nodded toward the couch. "Come and sit down, and stop worrying. Your father's right. Theo's old enough to take care of himself."

She moved reluctantly to sit, curling into the corner of the worn couch and pulling one of Gran's needlepoint pillows into her lap. Hugging it was vaguely comforting, like hugging Gran.

"I guess he is. But he'll always be the baby as far as I'm concerned. I'll always feel responsible."

Luke put a piece of split wood in the fireplace with as much concentration as he'd give to an annual report. The glow from the fire lit his profile, touching the frowning dark brows, highlighting his high cheekbones and determined jaw.

"I wouldn't know about that. I didn't have any brothers or sisters."

Before she could respond, he stood, shrugging as if shaking off the thought. For an instant she imagined he meant to come and sit next to her. Then he propped his elbow on the mantel, leaning against it and looking down into the flames.

"That must have been different, growing up an only child." She tried to imagine it. "Believe me, there were plenty of times when I could have done without the horde of Caldwell kids. Counting my cousins, there were seven of us, and that often seemed a few too many.''

''Why? I thought your family was picture perfect, Chloe Elizabeth.''

She couldn't tell whether that was mockery in his voice or not, and she hugged the pillow a little tighter. ''I guess I felt lost in the crowd. People would say, 'Now, which one are you?' as if I didn't have any identity of my own.''

Some emotion she couldn't interpret seemed to darken his eyes. ''That's nonsense.'' His voice roughened. ''They all love you, Chloe. Even I can see that.''

Tears stung, and she blinked rapidly. ''I've let them down. I should have done something about Theo, and I didn't.'' She bit her lip, trying to keep the tears from spilling over. ''This is my fault.''

''No, it's not.'' Luke shoved himself away from the mantel as if it took an effort. Two strides brought him across the hooked rug to stand in front of her. His body blocked out the light from the fire. ''It's not your fault.''

She shook her head, feeling the tears hot on her cheeks. ''You don't understand.''

''I understand that you're a good person,'' he said. ''I understand that you're beating yourself up over something that's not your fault.''

''It is my fault.'' She dashed away the tears impatiently. "Theo looked up to me the same way I looked up to the twins. I had a responsibility."

"That's who you are, isn't it, Chloe."

He sounded almost angry, as if she'd given the wrong answer to a question.

"Like it or not, you're a Caldwell. Everything you are is tied up with family."

"What's wrong with that?" Her own anger flared.

"Nothing. Everything."

Before she could guess what he was about, he grasped her hands and drew her upright. Gran's pillow tumbled to the floor.

"You're Chloe Elizabeth Caldwell." His voice had gentled, and his hands were warm and strong on her wrists. "I'm just figuring out who that is, after all this time."

She looked up at him and her breath caught. He was too close—his gaze on her face was too steady. If she let herself look into the depths of his eyes, she'd get lost and never find her way out. But she couldn't stop.

His hand lifted, very slowly, and he touched her cheek the way he had that morning. But this time he didn't pull away. She swayed toward him, as if caught in the tide.

His touch moved across her cheek gently, but it left heat in its wake. His fingers slid into her hair, tangling there. And then his lips found hers.

She couldn't move, couldn't think. She didn't need to think.

She slid her arms around him, feeling the warmth of his skin through the smooth cotton of his shirt. His arms were strong and protective, and he held her as if he'd never let go.

"Chloe." He breathed her name against her lips, then kissed her again.

This was the moment she'd dreamed about for years. The words pressed against her lips, demanding to be spoken. She couldn't fool herself any longer about her feelings. She loved him. She had to tell him she loved him—

The door crashed open, sending a flood of wind and water into the room.

Chapter Nine

Luke suddenly stood a foot away from her, and Chloe wasn't quite sure how that had happened. She was cold, either from the blast of wet air or the fact that she was no longer held in his embrace.

Theo halted on the doorstep, eyes wide, hair dripping. Then he started to leave.

Chloe's heart clenched at the thought of losing him again. She flew across the room, reaching him before he could pull the door shut. "No, Theo." She grabbed his arm, and his sweatshirt was soaked. "Get in here. Aren't you wet enough already?"

She didn't intend to sound scolding, but the response seemed natural, as if her mother's voice echoed in her head.

"Sorry." She hugged him quickly, and he felt stiff and cold in her arms. "I'm just so relieved to see you. You scared us half to death. Where have you been?''

Theo shrugged out of her hug, but he let her pull him into the room. ''Around. Can't a man be by himself in this family for a minute or two without everybody getting involved?''

She laughed a little shakily. ''Funny. I was just saying the same thing myself. Sometimes you get overwhelmed with Caldwells, don't you.''

She longed to hold him, but contented herself with brushing the wet hair out of his eyes.

He jerked away from her hand. ''It's not the same. You're not the baby.''

Be careful. Somehow she had to get through to him, convince him to go home. But she was weighted down by the sense of having failed him already.

She heard Luke's step behind her, and his hand brushed hers with a kind of wordless sympathy. ''Why don't you get rid of those wet clothes. None of us will be going anywhere until the weather improves.''

Theo seemed to look at that suggestion from every angle, his eyes wary. Then he nodded and yanked off the wet sweatshirt, letting it drop to the floor. A shiver ran through him. He seemed so young and vulnerable, standing there in his T-shirt and jeans.

''Theo—''

Theo shot her a glare that stopped her words. Theo wasn't the sweet little baby she'd rocked or the cuddly toddler who'd snuggled close to her for a story.

He'd turned into a gangly teenager, hovering on the line between boyhood and manhood. She longed to help him, longed to erase the disappointment hiding behind the bravado in his eyes, but she feared that she couldn't.

She had to try. "We were worried about you. Everyone was. That's natural, isn't it?"

She sensed Luke standing next to her, and it took an effort not to look at him. This wasn't his concern. This was Caldwell family business.

"I'm not a little kid anymore." Theo stalked across to the fireplace and kicked at the fire, sending a shower of sparks upward. "I don't need people telling me what to do. I can decide that for myself. You did."

She battled to keep her voice level. "I was a little older than you."

"You left." He threw the words at her. "You made your life somewhere else, where nobody tells you what to do. So don't you tell me."

Pain unfurled, closing her throat. She wanted to say something. But what could she tell him? He'd already decided she didn't have the right. "Theo..."

Luke's hands closed on her shoulders. "Chloe." His voice was low. "Didn't you say something about coffee?"

She knew her pain was written in her eyes. "I don't have time for that now."

"Yes, you do." His grasp tightened, insisting on her attention. "Go on, now. Make us some coffee.

We'll all feel better when we have something hot inside us."

Leave me alone with him. She could hear the words he didn't speak. *Let me try.*

When did she start hearing the things he didn't say aloud? She wanted to argue, but he couldn't do any worse than she seemed to be doing.

"All right. I'll have it ready in a few minutes." She tried sending him an unspoken message of her own. *Be careful. Be gentle with him.*

He nodded as if he understood, and squeezed her shoulders reassuringly. "Go ahead. We'll be fine."

Theo stood at the fireplace, his thin figure outlined against its glow. His weight hadn't caught up to his height yet, and the vulnerable curve of his neck made her heart ache. She blinked back the tears that stung her eyes and headed for the kitchen.

Once safely out of Theo's sight, she didn't have to hide her anguish. She closed the door, then leaned back against it. *Oh, Lord, what am I going to do?*

Was she pleading for answers about Theo? Or answers about Luke? She didn't seem to know. She pressed her hands against her cheeks. They still felt hot, as if Luke's kisses had left a permanent mark.

No. She pushed herself away from the door, reaching for the coffeepot. She couldn't think about Luke, about what his kisses meant, not now. If she started, she'd be overwhelmed, and right now she had to concentrate on Theo's problems. She'd already failed him once, and she couldn't do it again.

She put heavy white mugs on a battered tin tray, then stood holding it for a moment, sending up another prayer. *Please, Lord. Give me the words.*

Rain spattered against the kitchen window, reminding her of the tears she was determined not to shed. Theo was her brother. The responsibility was hers. She didn't expect any help from Luke.

She took a deep breath and started to push the door open. Then she heard Luke's voice and froze.

"...just don't think running away is the answer."

"You wouldn't say that if you knew anything about it." Theo sounded as stubborn as their father. "Guess you probably never had to run away in your life."

"Never?"

Luke's echo had an odd sound—one that would have warned her off in an instant. She held her breath. Should she go in? Or was it better to let whatever was happening between them run its course?

"I ran away more times than I can count—" Luke's voice had gone flat, and she had the impression he forced the words out.

"And I didn't have a place like this to run to, I can tell you."

"But I thought—"

"You thought I was born with a silver spoon in my mouth. Thought there was nothing in my life to run away from. Wrong on both counts."

She couldn't see him from where she stood with the door half open between them, and she wanted to.

She wanted to know why he'd said things to Theo that he hadn't said to her in six years.

"Tell me this, Theo." Luke's voice had firmed. "Did running away make the problem disappear?"

"Guess not." Theo's response was a sulky mumble.

"Most times it doesn't. Here's something I learned the hard way. A man doesn't run away. A man stays and faces trouble, no matter what it is. Running away—that's kid stuff."

Chloe clutched the tray, waiting for Theo to flare up at him or to run out the door. He did neither. She counted the seconds until she heard his long intake of breath.

"Guess maybe it's time I went home and talked to my daddy about this."

She pushed the door a little farther. She could see Luke's grave expression as he put his hand on Theo's shoulder.

"I think that would be a good idea," he said.

Chloe blinked rapidly as she tried to swallow the lump in her throat. Luke had done what she hadn't been able to do. He'd shown an insight she'd never have believed possible from him.

In fact, she still didn't believe it—not from the Luke Hunter she knew back at corporate headquarters. This was a different Luke Hunter. Maybe, given the man he'd shown her since they'd been on the island, she could even believe his kisses meant something.

She pushed the door the rest of the way open and carried the tray to the coffee table. "Coffee is ready now. Anyone want some?"

Theo stood, squaring his shoulders. "It's starting to clear some." He nodded toward the windows. "We ought to be getting home."

"Maybe so," she said, trying not to let emotion show in her tone.

She looked beyond her brother to Luke, knowing that everything in her heart must be clear in her eyes. He met her gaze with a look of perfect understanding.

Her breath stopped. They knew each other. They looked into the depths of each other's souls, and they understood each other. Whatever relationship they'd had in the past, it was transformed now beyond all recognition. There was no going back.

"There's my daddy."

Luke could hear the tension in Theo's voice as they approached the dock in front of the inn. He put a steadying hand on the boy's shoulder.

Chloe pulled back on the throttle, and the boat bounced over the waves. The setting sun touched her hair with gold as it painted the horizon in shades of crimson and orange.

"Red sky at night, sailor's delight." She nodded toward the sky. "Looks like it will be a good day tomorrow."

She was as tense as her little brother, he decided.

She just hid it a little better. All three of them watched her father's spare figure climb to the dock from the small boat and stand waiting.

Theo shot Luke an anguished look. "You...you're not going anyplace now, are you?"

Actually, he'd been planning to do a quick disappearing act. The Caldwell family problems were none of his business, and he certainly couldn't pose as an authority on what families were supposed to be.

But Theo seemed to need him, and Chloe was looking at him with perfect confidence that he wouldn't desert them. So he guessed he was staying.

Chloe eased the boat into position, then tossed a line to her father. He wrapped it without a word. There was a moment of awkward stillness. Then Luke pushed the boy gently toward the dock. They might as well get this over with.

The kid's tension was riding him now. He knew what several foster fathers had done to him for running away. He couldn't begin to guess how Chloe's father would react, but the next few minutes were bound to be painful.

Clayton Caldwell stood for an instant, his strong face impassive, looking at his son. Then he reached out and swept the boy into his arms. Theo went with a choked sob and clung to him as if holding to a rock in a storm.

Luke's throat went ridiculously dry. He cleared it,

then held out his hand to Chloe. "Maybe we should go up to the house."

An errant tear sparkled on her cheek, and Chloe brushed it away, nodding.

But as they climbed out onto the dock, Chloe's father put out a hand. "No. Stay." He looked from them to Theo. "I've got some explaining to do. You two went after your brother. I expect you've got a right to hear what I have to say."

"Daddy..." Chloe began to protest, but at her father's look she fell silent.

Clayton held his son at arm's length, hands on the boy's shoulders. "I was wrong, son. I shouldn't have told you no without explaining the whole thing. Reckon I've got a good reason to feel like I do about that yacht club crowd, but you've got a right to know why."

Luke felt Chloe shift uneasily. He reached out to put his arm around her waist, drawing her close to his side.

She looked startled for an instant, then leaned against him. He shouldn't hold her, he told himself, but Chloe probably needed a little support about now. It was the least he could do. The evening breeze fluttered her hair against his cheek.

Clayton leaned against a post, his bad leg extended stiffly, and stared down at the worn planks beneath his feet. "I was just about your age, boy, the summer it started. Lines between islanders and summer people were even stricter then. They didn't associate with us, and we stayed clear of them except for working. I figured that was okay, until I met Emily.''

''Emily?'' Chloe sounded startled, maybe even confused. Apparently she'd never heard this story before, either.

''Emily Brandeis.'' The lines in Clayton's face deepened. ''Wealthy folks, here for the summer. Kind of people who wouldn't talk to islanders, 'cept to give an order. But Emily was different.'' His expression softened suddenly, giving the impression of a much younger man.

''First love,'' Chloe said gently.

He nodded. ''Guess so. I was crazy about her, and her about me, I thought. Trouble was, my brother liked her, too.''

Could this possibly be the cause of the rift between the brothers? Luke would have expected a quarrel over a summer love to heal long ago, but clearly Clayton had more to say.

''We fought about it. Seems like we fought about everything that summer. Maybe I was getting tired of pulling Jefferson out of trouble all the time. Anyway, we had to keep it a secret, seeing Emily, or there'd have been trouble.'' He took a deep breath.

Luke felt Chloe tense. Did she suspect what was coming? He sensed the hurt radiating from her, and he tightened his arm around her, feeling a ridiculous need to protect her from pain.

''Emily was…'' He paused, mouth softening a little. ''She was different from anyone I'd ever known, or Jeff had known, for that matter. Seemed like she had everything, but she loved it here, loved the island, especially loved Chloe's dolphin in the chapel. Said she'd like to take it home with her, to remind her of that summer.''

"You didn't." Chloe's voice rang with absolute certainty.

"No, sugar, I didn't take the dolphin. I wouldn't." His jaw hardened. "There was a party one night, toward the end of summer, out on Angel Isle. Emily went with me. Jeff was there a while, then gone, but I didn't miss him. I had Emily. Then Emily's daddy showed up with some of his friends."

"What happened?" Theo's face was white. Maybe he knew the answer, too.

"Pushed me around pretty good. I fell." He patted his leg. "That's how I got this stiff leg. Broke in a couple of places, and it never did heal right." He shrugged. "I never saw Emily again. And the next day the dolphin was missing."

Chloe sounded shocked. "I never knew that was when you hurt your leg. But Uncle Jefferson wouldn't have taken the dolphin, would he?"

Her father looked tired. "I didn't want to think so, either, but the dolphin was gone. And I know it was Jefferson who told her father about Emily and me. He'd do anything to get on the good side of those people. Anything." He touched his leg again. "Never, ever said he was sorry."

Chloe slipped out of his grasp, going to put a comforting hand on her father's arm. "Did you ever talk to him about it?"

Clayton shoved himself away from the post. "I spent my life covering up for things Jeff did, even taking the blame when I had to. I was the older one—I figured it was my job. But that night was the last straw. Jefferson picked his life for himself. He'd say he's got it all—the business, the big house. What I think doesn't matter to him."

"But, Daddy—"

"Leave it, Chloe-girl." He shook his head. "Point is, nothing good has ever come to this family from that yacht club crowd. Look at your sister. If Miranda hadn't been working there, she never would have run off and married the wrong man." He focused on Theo. "But it's your decision, boy. If you figure you're old enough to work there, then you must be old enough to handle it. I leave it up to you."

Theo seemed to grow an inch or two. "Thank you, Daddy."

"Guess we'd best go tell your mother and Gran you're all right." Clayton put his hand on his son's shoulder, and together they started up toward the house.

Luke stood with Chloe, watching them go, and his throat hurt with longing. Longing for—what? He'd never known a father. How could he feel homesick for something he'd never had?

He tried to shake off the feeling. "Looks like they're going to be all right."

"Yes." Chloe's voice was soft, and she leaned against him without prompting. "Thank you, Luke."

He shouldn't be enjoying this so much. "For what? I didn't do anything."

"You made Theo see, when I couldn't. You helped me bring him home—"

Her hair brushed his cheek as she tilted her head to look up at him. Something so intense that it frightened him shone in her eyes.

"You talked to him from your heart."

"Most people would deny I even have one."

Her smile trembled on the edge of tears. "Most people would be wrong. Most people haven't seen the Luke Hunter I've seen since we've been here on the island."

It came to him then. He cared about her. He cared about Chloe Caldwell, with a longing that twisted his heart.

He'd told himself that she couldn't ever be right for him. That she couldn't be the woman he needed by his side to get where he wanted to go.

Now he looked at the truth, and it didn't give him any comfort. The truth was, he wasn't the right man for her. He knew without asking what kind of man Chloe Caldwell needed—a man who'd put faith and family before anything else.

He couldn't be that man. He never would be, and it hurt.

"Are you sure you don't mind picking up Miranda?" Chloe glanced at him from the passenger side of the rental car the next day, her expression a little wary.

"Of course not." He heard the edge in his voice and wanted to bite his tongue. No wonder Chloe looked wary. He been acting like a bear with a sore paw all day. He had to put some distance between Chloe and himself. Those moments when he'd held her, kissed her—that had been a mistake. He knew that, even if she didn't.

He'd intended this trip to the county seat to be the moment he told her about Angel Isle and enlisted her help. It was past time. He couldn't keep pretending to be interested in all the other sites she pointed out, when he'd already given Dalton his enthusiastic endorsement of Angel Isle.

But somehow the moment had never seemed right, and the words remained unsaid. Maybe the truth was that he doubted his ability to get Chloe on his side over this.

She still looked at him doubtfully.

"It's fine." He forced some warmth into his tone as he turned onto the main street of Beaufort. "Just give me directions."

"Down another block or two, on the right." She frowned. "Sorry the traffic is so bad. Beaufort's a visitor magnet this time of year."

"I can see why." Quaint shops and restaurants lined the waterfront; boats moved up and down the channel. Farther down the street he could see a row of graceful antebellum mansions, lawns abloom with azaleas. "What's the name of the place we're looking for?"

"Sonlight Center. Son with an *O*. It's a mission, really. Miranda volunteers there one day a week."

"What kind of mission?" Something tightened inside him.

"Youth-oriented." Chloe leaned forward, looking for the sign. "They run after-school programs. And in the summer they bring city kids out here, give them a taste of low-country life." She turned toward him, silky hair swinging across her cheek, eyes serious. "You wouldn't believe the kind of lives some of those kids come from."

Wouldn't I, Chloe? Tension skittered along his nerves. *Wouldn't I?*

Luckily Chloe spotted the place before he had to answer. "There. There's a parking space right in front."

He pulled to the curb.

When he didn't turn off the engine, she raised her eyebrows.

"Don't you want to come in with me?"

No, he didn't. But he probably couldn't avoid it. He switched off the ignition with a sense of fatality. He was about to be reminded of things he'd rather forget.

And it was every bit as bad as he had thought it would be. No quick escape. Miranda insisted on showing them everything, from the cramped offices to the after-school tutoring sessions to the gym.

Sneakers squeaked on the polished floor, shouts echoed from the ceiling. A gang of boys elbowed one another for the ball. It bounced toward him, and he grabbed it automatically, then fed it back to the lean, gray-haired man whose whistle tangled with the cross around his neck.

"Thanks." He gave them a friendly wave, then charged down the court.

"That's Pastor Mike." Affection filled Miranda's voice. "He still thinks he's young enough to keep up with the boys."

Like the Rev. An emotion he didn't want to identify pooled in Luke's stomach. Guilt, was that what it was?

He kept the smile pinned to his face through sheer willpower. He'd been one of those kids once—edgy, angry, taking his aggression out on the basketball court instead of the street, because one man had cared enough to try to reach him.

He took a breath, trying to still the tumult inside him. He wasn't that boy now. He hadn't been for a long time.

Coming here had been a mistake. Coming to Chloe's island had been a mistake. The place and the people confused him. They reminded him of the past he wanted to forget, and at the same time made him long for a future he could never have.

Chapter Ten

"All right, Chloe Elizabeth." Miranda turned from the dishwasher where she was stacking the breakfast dishes the next morning. "Out with it. What's going on between you and your sweetheart?"

Chloe tried to keep her face impassive as she put down the coffeepot she'd just carried in from the dining room. "Nothing's going on. What do you mean?"

"Don't tell me that, sugar, 'cause I don't believe it." Miranda leaned back against the counter. "You haven't been gone long enough to learn how to fool me. I can tell something's wrong. Something's been wrong."

"Nothing's wrong." *Nothing except that when we were on Angel Isle looking for Theo, he kissed me as I'd never been kissed before. He made me feel as if he could love me. And then he turned it all off as if it had never been.*

But she couldn't say any of that to Miranda, no matter how much she might long to confide in her sister. "Your imagination's working overtime."

Miranda looked at her steadily. "I don't think so. That night you brought Theo home, you walked in here looking…transformed." Her voice softened on the word, her face suddenly misty, as if remembering. "But yesterday Luke went off to Savannah by himself, and you've been moping around like all the sunshine went out of your life."

Transformed. The word echoed in her heart. Maybe she had been, for a short time, but it hadn't lasted. Luke had put a wall between them. And she couldn't even count on leaving in a few days, as she'd expected. He'd said the proposal for Dalton wasn't ready yet, and insisted they stay longer. Her family was too happy to have them home to probe her reasons.

"Miranda…" She wanted to say something that would put her sister off the track, but she couldn't, not when Miranda looked at her with truth and expectation in her green eyes. "I can't talk about it, okay? We just have to work it out ourselves." *Or not.*

Miranda's expression dissolved into sympathy, and she gave Chloe a quick hug. "Oh, honey, I'm sorry I poked my nose in. But if you want to talk, you know I'm here."

"I know." Chloe hugged her back, eyes filling with tears. She'd like nothing better than to confide in her sister, but the promise she hadn't wanted to make held her fast. "I will."

"Well." Miranda wiped her eyes with the back of her hand. "Enough of this foolishness. We've got to get the food packed up to take over to Gran's, or Mom will regret leaving us in charge of it."

"Right. I just hope she's keeping Gran from doing too much. If anyone can, it's Mom."

She busied herself putting ice in the cooler, relieved that the noise she was making meant she didn't have to talk.

The situation with Luke was too difficult to discuss. His withdrawal could mean only one thing— that he regretted what had happened between them.

She'd told herself that a hundred times over, but it still cut her heart into pieces. She frowned at the blueberry pies she was loading into the pie carrier. She didn't have a choice in the matter. Luke had made his decision clear without saying a word. Now all she could do was try to stay as detached as he did.

If she could. She took a deep breath. She had to. And that would make it much easier to tell him. Another little sliver of her heart seemed to break off. Like it or not, her mind was made up. Her days as Luke Hunter's right hand were numbered. She wasn't going back to Chicago with him.

"The way you're frowning, sugar, anyone would think you hated blueberry pies."

Miranda's teasing drawl roused her, and she managed a smile.

"Just wondering if these will be enough. Putting the new roof on Gran's house is going to be hungry work."

"I've been hiding a chocolate cake in the pantry," Miranda said. "Is Luke going along today?"

Chloe's heart clenched. Luke had to have heard the rest of the family talking about the big workday to put the roof on, but he'd surely make an excuse.

"I think he has some work to do today."

The words had barely left her mouth when she heard a clatter of feet in the hallway, announcing her brothers' arrival. "Don't get out of here without carrying something," she called, only too aware of her brothers' propensity for getting out of anything they'd think of as "women's work."

"Come on, Chloe." Daniel pushed the door open. "We've got the tools to take. Can't you manage that?"

"You're going to eat, aren't you?" A glimpse of Luke over her brother's shoulder made her words tart. "You can help tote."

Luke eased into the kitchen behind her brothers. "I'll be glad to carry the pies. That should give me first chance at them."

"You…" Chloe looked up at him, and the rest of her question seemed to shrivel in the need just to see him, to store up enough memories to last her when he was gone.

"Luke's coming to help." Daniel pounded Luke's shoulder in a friendly blow that should have staggered him.

Luke just smiled, apparently used to her brothers by this time. "I can't miss the chance to repay your grandmother for her hospitality. I'm glad to help."

Miranda began loading them up with things to carry. In the inevitable bustle as they started out the door, Chloe caught Luke's arm.

His skin was warm under her fingers, and she snatched them away before she could give in to the longing to hold on to him.

"You don't have to do this," she said in an undertone. "I'm sure you have work to do."

"No." His intent gaze stilled her protest. "There's nothing I'd rather do than this, Chloe. Are you ready?"

She had no choice but to follow him out the door, wondering how she'd possibly manage to keep her resolution to stay detached, when just a look from him was enough to put her fractured heart back together again.

By the time they reached Gran's, the rest of the clan had assembled. Her cousin Adam was already putting a ladder against the side of the house, while her mother and Gran set jugs of ice water and sweet tea on the picnic table. Her father and David conferred over a stack of shingles, while Uncle Jefferson hefted a toolbox from his truck.

Everyone had something to do. Even Sammy had been assigned to take water, nails, whatever was needed to the workers. Everyone had a part, she told herself, except Luke. He didn't belong here.

Did she? The thought popped into her mind so suddenly that it sent a wave of panic through her, making her feel the way she had when she'd been ten and caught in a riptide. Daddy had pulled her out that time, but he couldn't help now. She had to work this one out for herself.

"Are they talking?" Luke's baritone, soft in her ear, made her jump, then sent a tendril of warmth curling through her.

Stop it, she ordered, not sure whether she was talking to herself or Luke. She followed the direction of Luke's nod and saw that the group around the shingles had been joined by Uncle Jefferson.

"I don't know. I wish…" She let that die, because there was no point in confiding in Luke—not anymore.

"I know."

His voice was so soft it couldn't have reached any of the others, so close his breath stirred across her cheek. He enclosed her hand in his and squeezed it gently.

"I know what you wish, Chloe."

"You really don't have to stay, you know," she

said in desperation. "You won't want to work up on the roof."

"I won't?" He lifted an eyebrow. "Why not, Chloe? Do you think I'm afraid of heights, just because I'm afraid of the water? That's kind of insulting, isn't it?"

"I didn't mean that. You know I didn't." Maybe if she pretended she was snapping at one of her brothers, this would go easier. "But I'm sure you've never done work like this before. It's hard." Well, that sounded even more insulting. Maybe she should just keep quiet.

"And hot, and dirty. Especially ripping off the old shingles to get down to something solid."

Her surprise had to show in her face. "You do know something about it."

He shrugged, picking up a pair of work gloves from the picnic table. "I worked construction one summer. There's nothing here I haven't seen before—"

He stopped, looking at her with something in his eyes she couldn't interpret.

"Except maybe you, Chloe."

He walked swiftly to the ladder, and a moment later was deep in conversation with her cousin.

She took a deep breath, hoping nothing was showing on her face to be noted and dissected by these people who knew her so well. What had he meant? Why had he even come today? It just made things more difficult.

She lifted the heavy picnic hamper. She had to stop thinking about him, about the possibility of a future that wasn't going to be. But each time she made a decision, Luke did something or said something to change it, leaving her caught once again on the painful edge between resignation and hope.

"Bring that hamper over here, Chloe Elizabeth." Gran called to her from the kitchen doorway. "Let me see if anything needs to go in the icebox."

Her grandmother had a refrigerator, but it would always be an "icebox" to her.

"The cold things are in the cooler, Gran." Chloe obediently took the hamper into the kitchen. At least there she wouldn't have to see Luke. Maybe she could stop thinking about him.

"What's this I hear about your young man?" Cousin Phoebe lifted the hamper lid to peek into each bowl.

Chloe suppressed a sigh. "I don't know, Cousin Phoebe. What did you hear?"

Phoebe's nose twitched. "Elvira Thompson's girl saw him in Savannah yesterday. Wouldn't you like to know what he was doing?"

"He had some work to do there." Work he hadn't asked her to share.

"Not unless he's working in a jewelry store," Phoebe announced triumphantly. She leaned on a chair back, waiting for the exclamations sure to follow.

No one disappointed her. Gran, Miranda, Chloe's

mother—all pressed around her. Chloe's heart sank. Whatever innocent purpose had taken Luke there was sure to be twisted out of all recognition.

"A jewelry store." Gran savored the words. "She didn't happen to see what he bought, did she?"

Phoebe shook her head with an expression of regret. "She couldn't get close enough for that, but it was a small box. She saw him put it into his pocket." Phoebe paused. "A ring-size box. Looks like our Chloe's going to get herself engaged."

He had to stop doing that. Luke climbed the ladder Chloe's cousin held for him, only a fraction of his attention on the rungs. He had to stop letting things slip where Chloe was concerned.

How much had he shown Chloe in the past week that he hadn't shown anyone else in the past fifteen years? He didn't want to count.

From the day he'd started college, he'd set out to reinvent himself. Reverend Tom and his foundation had given him the means to do that, and he'd gone about it with iron determination. He would turn himself into one of them—one of those favored few who took achievement and power for granted. And a big piece of his plan had involved keeping where he'd come from a secret.

That had never been a problem, until now. The persona he'd adopted had become a second skin. Until Chloe and her family started peeling it away.

It had to stop. A momentary panic washed over

him. No one back in Chicago knew the truth about his background. What if they found out?

"You okay?" Chloe's cousin balanced next to him on the roof edge.

"Fine." Luke took the crowbar the other man held out. Adam, he reminded himself. This was the Caldwell who ran the shipyard. Tall, like all the Caldwell men, but with dark brown hair and a pair of steady gray eyes. "Let's get this done."

He shoved the pry bar under a stretch of fraying shingles. They came up with a satisfying rip. He'd concentrate on what he was doing. He wouldn't think about Chloe, because if he did he'd have to look at the future, and for the first time in fifteen years he wasn't perfectly certain what it held.

The morning fell into a rhythm that gradually displaced the turmoil in his mind. Chloe had been right about one thing—this was the most physical work he'd done in a long time. Playing handball at the club might keep him in shape for the life he normally led, but it didn't strain the muscles like this.

He and Adam worked side by side along the stretch of roof, with David and Daniel working a few feet above them. The steady, repetitive movements were oddly soothing, as soothing as the soft Southern voices teasing each other with the ease of long familiarity.

"Is that all you boys have gotten done?" Chloe's voice came from the top of the ladder.

"Fine talk from someone's who's been down there

lolling in the shade, drinking lemonade,'' Daniel teased.

Chloe pulled the brim of a baseball cap down over her forehead. Her hair, more gold than brown after her days in the sun, curled around it. ''Hey, it's a dirty job, but somebody has to do it. You can go down and listen to Cousin Phoebe's gallbladder story, if you want.''

Daniel shuddered. ''No, thanks. You'd best get back down there, Chloe-girl.''

''Are you kidding? I'm here to give you slow-pokes a hand. Daddy wants all the old shingles off before we stop for lunch.''

''You taking Theo's place?'' Adam asked, wiping his forehead with the back of his arm, then putting his cap back on.

If Theo's absence while working at the yacht club bothered Chloe, she didn't show it.

''I'm faster than Theo is.'' She clambered across the roof as easily as she hopped onto the boat. ''Give me that pry bar. I'll loosen while you throw the shingles down.''

Smiling, Adam held the bar out of her reach. ''You'd best help your beau, sugar. After all, the two of you should get used to working together.''

For an instant Chloe's face seemed to freeze, as if time had stopped. Luke shoved the pry bar under an edge of shingles.

''Here, Chloe. I'll pry them up, and you toss them

over the side. Let's see if we can beat your brothers to the end of the row.''

That set David and Daniel off, and under the cover of their ribbing he studied Chloe's face. It didn't tell him anything, and he'd thought he could interpret her every expression. She frowned at the shingles as she pulled them free and tossed them over the side. She didn't meet his gaze.

Maybe she was as confused as he was about what was happening between them. Maybe she sensed, as he did, that they could never go back to the way they'd been before.

Probably that didn't matter to Chloe, he told himself. After all, she had roots. She had a place where she belonged, where her people went back for generations. Four generations of Caldwells worked together at that very moment, putting a new roof on a house that had stood on this same spot for two hundred years or so. His carefully created facade seemed a flimsy, Cracker Jack box thing in comparison.

Sink your roots deep in the Word. Reverend Tom's voice came from nowhere, echoing in his mind. *That's where you belong, son.*

The Rev had called all of them ''son.'' All of the ragtag gang of losers he'd taken off the streets had been ''son'' to him. It hadn't meant anything personal.

He seemed to see again Clayton Caldwell and Theo, walking toward the welcoming lights of the big old house, the man's hand on the boy's shoulder.

A shiver ran along his skin in spite of the heat. That was what he'd always wanted. What he'd never had. He hadn't realized how much he missed it until he came here.

"All right." Adam reached the end of the row. "We did it." He gave Luke a friendly buffet on the shoulder. "Good job, Luke. Time for a lunch break."

It was a simple gesture, nothing to make a fuss about. But suddenly he felt accepted. As if he, too, could belong here.

Nonsense. He dropped the pry bar carefully down to the grass beneath. He didn't have any need to belong here, nor any longing to. He belonged back in Chicago, in the world he'd created for himself.

He started down the ladder, trying not to be aware of Chloe, following him down. This was her fault, bringing him here, making him question things he'd taken for granted for years.

His feet touched the ground and he reached up automatically to help Chloe. She hopped down the last few rungs, and his arms closed around her.

He heard the quick intake of her breath, felt the soft, warm, aliveness of her fill his arms, and all his certainty slipped away. Just the touch of her, the memory of her gentleness and loyalty, and his careful plans to keep things normal between them slipped crazily out of his control.

Chapter Eleven

"Chloe Elizabeth." Gran grabbed Chloe with one hand and Luke with the other. "I want you and Luke to do something for me before you go home."

Chloe was instantly wary. Anything Gran wanted them to do had *matchmaking* written all over it, and the situation between her and Luke was difficult enough already.

But Luke bent toward Gran attentively. "What is it, Gran? Anything for you."

Gran dimpled up at him. "Well, now, it's just so simple it won't take any time at all. And I'm sure you're wanting to have another look at the chapel, anyway, since..."

"Gran, we really need to get home and shower. Roofing's a dirty job." If Gran had finished that sentence, it would undoubtedly have had something to do with a wedding that wasn't going to take place.

"Now, Chloe, I need the flowers taken into the chapel for services tomorrow. You can surely stay long enough to do that."

"Of course we can." Luke patted her hand. "And I'd love to see the chapel more closely."

Her family's need to matchmake had passed the humorous point. And as for those engagement rumors—Chloe didn't even want to think about that. She suppressed a sigh. Gran was just being Gran. It wasn't her fault that Chloe was so uncertain right now about what Luke felt.

"Okay, what do you want us to take?"

"Thank you, sugar. It's too bad the azaleas are about through, but my early lilac is blooming its heart out. And there are a few tulips left that will look nice with them. I'll just get the bucket and clippers for you."

Chloe had to smile at the expression on Luke's face when her grandmother bustled off. "You didn't anticipate picking and arranging flowers, did you?"

His face relaxed in a disarming grin. "I have a lot of talents, Chloe, but flower arranging isn't among them. You'll have to do that part."

"Seems to me you're the one who jumped into this. Maybe it's time you acquired a new skill." Chloe went to take the bucket and clippers from her grandmother. She'd give her next Christmas bonus to see Luke Hunter doing flower arrangements.

Then she sobered. If she followed through with her decision not to go back to Chicago, she wouldn't be there for the Christmas bonus. If she was lucky, she might get an anonymous printed card from Luke.

"Here's the lilac," she announced unnecessarily, as Gran went back into the house, closing the door firmly as if to remind them that they were alone.

Chloe handed Luke the clippers. "Why don't you cut a few of those flowering branches from the top, and I'll get the tulips."

"Come on, Chloe." He snipped a heavily laden branch of the old-fashioned white lilacs that were the envy of every gardener on the island. "This is a small thing to do to make your grandmother happy."

She'd heard that rationale before, and look where it had landed her. She cringed away from telling him about Cousin Phoebe's little bombshell. Maybe he'd never have to know. "You won't say that when the twins have used up all the hot water with their showers."

When they'd filled the bucket, she led the way into the chapel. Luke braced his hand against the weathered wood of the door to hold it open for her. "Isn't the chapel ever locked?"

"Not during the day. It is locked at night, since…"

"Since the dolphin disappeared," he finished for her.

She nodded, walking toward the heavy brass vases that stood on either side of the pulpit. "That's when folks realized crime could strike even here. You can fill those with water from the bucket, if you're sure you don't want to do the arranging part.''

Luke smiled, shaking his head. He put the flowers on the paper she spread out, then poured water carefully into the vases. "How long ago was the chapel built? It looks as if it's been here forever.''

"Just about.'' Chloe put a branch of lilac into the vase, trying to defeat its natural tendency to flop over. "The sanctuary was built first, back in the late 1700s, and the church school rooms added later. In those days, the islands had a kind of circuit-rider preacher, though he went by boat, not horseback. That's why they called it St. Andrew's Chapel, rather than church. And St. Andrew, because he was a fisherman.''

"The islands were pretty isolated in those days, I guess.'' Luke walked slowly from one stained-glass window to another.

"Not only then. The bridge to the mainland wasn't built until the 1960s. Before that, folks had to be self-sufficient here.''

He turned to look at her. "They still are, aren't they?''

His steady gaze made her uncomfortable. "I guess.'' Was she self-sufficient? Or had she lost that when she left the island? Maybe she'd never really had it. Maybe she needed to come back to find it.

"Where was the dolphin?''

She indicated the shelf reluctantly.

Luke touched the empty bracket, as if it would

give him an image of the dolphin. "All this time," he murmured.

"My father didn't have anything to do with it," she said instantly.

"No." His frowning gaze met hers. "I'm sure he didn't, Chloe. But he's been keeping quiet about it. And you can't say it hasn't hurt him, at least, even if no one else was hurt."

That was more people wisdom than she'd expected from Luke, and it stilled her snappish response. "I suppose so," she said slowly. "I'm afraid the first Chloe isn't too happy with her descendants, if she knows."

He came to stand next to her, looking at the flower arrangements. The red tulips stood sentinel among the flowing white lilacs. "Nice job." He frowned. "If any part of your grandmother's story was true, that Chloe was a remarkable woman."

"Strong women." The words felt bitter in her mouth. "The Caldwells are known for strong women. Gran, my mother, Miranda—they're all good examples."

"And Chloe?"

Her gaze slid away from his. "I'm afraid the strain ran a little thin when it got to me. I can't live up to all of that." She shrugged, not knowing why she was saying this to him, but finding it impossible to keep the words back. "I guess that's really why I left the island in the first place. I needed to find someplace to belong where no one expected that much of me."

She stopped, horrified at herself. Why on earth had she said that to Luke? Exposing her emotions to him was just too dangerous. Luke probably didn't know it, but he had the power to wound her with nothing more than a look. And she'd just made him a present of her most carefully guarded secret.

Luke discovered he was holding his breath, and he let it out slowly. Chloe had opened her heart to him in a way he'd never expected, probably never experienced. She'd let him see into her soul, and he couldn't kid himself that she did that easily.

He faced a choice, and the silence grew between them as his mind veered from one to the other. His natural tendency was to say something neutral, something polite, something that by its very nature denied the importance of what Chloe had done. That would preserve the boss-secretary relationship between them.

Or he could answer her as honestly as she had spoken. That was dangerous. That would open some part of him to her, exposing vulnerabilities he didn't care to admit.

But it was too late, wasn't it? They could never go back to the way things had been before. They could only go forward.

He took her hand. It was small in his, but square and capable. ''You're underestimating yourself, Chloe.'' He couldn't stop at that. He had to find the words that would take the hurt from those golden-brown eyes. "And leaving didn't work, anyway, did it? As long as you had to stay away to prove your independence, you weren't really independent."

She frowned as if assessing his words. Her lashes swept down, veiling her eyes.

"So coming back showed me for a fraud, is that it?"

"No!" He tightened his grip. That was the last thing he wanted her to feel. "Coming back showed you that you never needed to go away at all. I didn't know who you were back in Chicago, do you understand that? It was only after we came here, after I saw you on your island, that I understood the real Chloe."

She focused on the flowers, as if she wasn't ready to meet his eyes. "I've always thought I should be more like Miranda and my mother—strong, serene, a calm center no matter what's happening around them."

"There are different kinds of strength, Chloe Elizabeth." He touched her stubborn chin, lifting it so he could see her eyes. "Your mother and sister are admirable women, but I suspect you take after your grandmother, instead. Feisty, loyal, determined. You can't tell me that's not something to be proud of."

A flood of color brightened her cheeks. "If I believed that, I couldn't ask for anything better."

"Believe it." Warning bells were going off in his mind but he suppressed them ruthlessly. "You're a special person, Chloe. Never forget that. I won't."

"Thank you." The words were whispered.

The moment seemed to stretch out infinitely. He could smell the sweetness of the lilacs, see dust motes floating in the shaft of colored light from the stained-glass windows, count every freckle on Chloe's sun-kissed skin. The silent chapel was caught in time, as if it could as easily be a hundred years ago, or tomorrow.

Chloe moved finally, breaking the spell. "We... we'd better go. My mother will wonder what happened to us."

He followed her up the aisle, pondering just what *had* happened to him here. They paused on the shaded walk while Chloe pulled the door closed. He caught her hand when she would have walked on.

"Let's not have dinner with your family tonight."

She looked up, startled. "What do you mean?"

"I mean, I'd like to have a little private time with my make-believe sweetheart, if that's all right with you." Again he had to suppress his built-in warning system. "There must be some restaurant where we can have a quiet dinner."

"I guess I can find one."

There was a question in her eyes. "We can talk business, if you like," he offered.

"Can we?" The dimple at the corner of her mouth made its appearance. "That would be a treat."

"I thought you'd like that." He took her hand. What he'd said was true enough, although he hadn't thought of it until then. They should talk business, just a little. It was past time for him to tell her his decision about Angel Isle.

But that wasn't why he wanted to go out alone with her, he knew perfectly well. He wanted to prolong those moments when they seemed able to see into each other's hearts. Dangerous or not, he wanted that.

They walked toward her grandmother's house, hands linked between them. He had to be out of his mind.

He didn't care.

"Wow." Daniel leaned against the door to Chloe's room, widening his eyes in exaggerated admiration. "Chloe's all dressed up, must be a special night."

David appeared next to him, his gaze softening as he looked at her. "Nice."

"Nice, indeed," Miranda scoffed, fluffing the skirt of the new yellow dress she'd insisted Chloe wear for her dinner with Luke. "Our Chloe is a beautiful woman. Can't help it if you two are too dumb to notice, heah."

The familiar Gullah word made Chloe smile in spite of the bad case of nerves she was having. All of them had known a smattering of Gullah, the language of the sea islands, since they'd started to talk. Hearing it in Miranda's soft voice made her feel a part of the endless island life again.

The twins went on down the stairs, and she heard

their joking voices continue in Gullah through the hall and out to the porch. Luke would wonder what on earth they were speaking.

If she came home to stay, if she told Luke she wouldn't be returning to Chicago and her job, this would be her life again. Could she do that? Could she sever all ties to her Chicago existence, just like that?

She wasn't sure. But she was sure that she couldn't go back to the way things had been between them. She couldn't be Luke's faithful right hand and ignore the fact that she loved him.

"Luke's waiting for you, honey." Miranda gave her a little push toward the hall.

Luke was waiting. She tried to calm the tension that bounced along her nerves. She couldn't go on this way, pretending.

She'd tell him. Tonight she'd tell him that she was considering staying here when he went back. If things had changed between them, if he'd begun to care about her, if his kiss had meant anything, surely that would bring it out.

She started down the stairs, the soft silk swishing against her legs. Her stomach twisted, and she felt as if she were fifteen again, going down these same stairs to greet her first date.

She had to know. One way or the other, she had to know.

Luke, bending over the puzzle Sammy was working on, looked up at her step. His eyes met hers, and she nearly missed the next stair. That stunned expression in his deep blue eyes had to mean something, didn't it? The thought floated her down the rest of the flight.

He came to her, holding out his hand, something that might have been a question in his eyes.

"Ready?"

She nodded, suddenly having nothing to say. The thought of telling him she wasn't going back seemed impossible. Maybe it was unnecessary. He might say—

"I don't know why y'all are going someplace for dinner. Gramma is fixing chicken tonight. You oughta stay here with us."

Miranda, who'd followed Chloe down the stairs, smiled at her small son. "They want to be by themselves for a change."

"But they can—"

Miranda put her hand gently over his mouth. "Enough, sugar. 'Bye, you two." She gave them a knowing smile. "Y'all have fun now, you hear?"

Luke opened the door. "Your carriage awaits, m'lady."

Sure her cheeks were as red as Gran's tulips, Chloe went through the door.

Once they were in the car, it should have been better. At least they were away from her family, with their obvious expectation that something special would happen tonight. They probably imagined that

Luke had an engagement ring hidden in the pocket of his navy slacks.

She knew better. Maybe that had been admiration in his eyes when she'd come down the steps; maybe he had enjoyed kissing her. But when it came to rings and wedding bells, Luke would marry with his eyes on the prize he wanted. That meant money and power, not a girl-next-door type with no prospects.

"Looks as if there are more people around town." Luke stopped at Caldwell Cove's only traffic light.

"The season's perking up as the weather gets warmer. Easter will really kick it off." He was probably thinking about the potential for a Dalton resort in the area. "Places like the Crab House, where we're going tonight, will extend their hours as things get busier."

Luke nodded, a frown creasing his forehead. Calculating the possibilities? She didn't know.

"Turn in here." She leaned forward, indicating the crushed-shell parking area of the Crab House. "Sorry, I didn't want you to miss the turn. What were you saying?"

He just shook his head, pulling into a space next to the dock. "This looks like the real thing."

"That it is." Chloe slid out, standing for a moment to drink in the scene. The fishing boats at the docks, their nets lifted, were old friends. "This is a working dock. When they tell you the seafood is fresh here, they mean it was swimming in the ocean a few hours ago."

Luke's hand closed around hers in a gesture that

had begun to feel natural. "So what are we eating tonight?"

"Shrimp, oysters, crab, or the day's catch. And the she-crab soup is the best you're ever going to taste, so don't miss that." Chloe inhaled the salty, fishy aroma of the docks. "Come on, let's see what's on the menu."

They sat at a table overlooking the sound, and the familiar land-and-waterscape reminded Chloe that she had planned to tell Luke she intended to stay. But somehow the moments ticked by, and the words never quite came out.

"You were right." Luke leaned back in his chair after the soup course. "The she-crab soup was delectable. What makes it so good?"

"Low-country secrets," she said, teasing. "You don't want me to betray them, do you?"

He reached across the small table to put his hand over hers. "We're on the same team," he said. "That's not betraying, is it?"

She shook her head, smiling. Somehow she didn't think being on the same team meant quite as much to Luke as it did to her. "My mother's promised to give me her recipe as a wedding present."

"That's almost worth getting married for." He squeezed her fingers, then reached toward his pocket. "By the way, I have something for you."

He pulled out a small jeweler's box, setting it on the table between them. She read the name of the Savannah jeweler on the lid, and her heart nearly stopped.

Don't be silly, she told herself fiercely. *It's not*

*what the family imagines. You're not foolish enough
to think that.*

She had to clear her throat so she could speak.
''What is it?''

''Something that made me think of you.'' He
pushed the box toward her with one finger. ''Go
ahead, open it.''

She reached out slowly, trying not to think, not to
imagine. She pressed the latch, and the lid flipped
up. Inside, a gold dolphin attached to a chain as fine
as a cobweb nestled on a bed of white satin. Her
throat closed; she couldn't say a word.

''What's wrong? Don't you like it?''

She blinked rapidly to keep tears from spilling
over. ''It's beautiful,'' she said carefully. ''You
shouldn't have.''

''I wanted to.'' He lifted it from the box, and it
dangled from his fingers, glinting in the candlelight.
''Let me fasten it for you.''

She turned her back to him, closing her eyes when
his fingers brushed the nape of her neck. The necklace was featherlight, and the dolphin seemed to
warm where it touched her skin.

''Thank you,'' she whispered. ''I love it.''

She did love it. It wasn't Luke's fault that her heart
yearned for something else.

She couldn't do this any longer. This evening had
to come to a close now. ''Maybe we should—''

''Look—''

She followed the direction of Luke's gaze, relieved
that he wasn't looking at her. The sun had slipped
lower, hiding behind the clouds that massed on the

mainland horizon. Then, quite suddenly, the color began to change. Gray clouds tinged with lavender, then mauve, then pink, the colors streaking across the darkening sky until the whole horizon glowed.

"If you saw that in a painting, it would look artificial." Luke's voice was soft.

"God's handiwork," she said, her own words just as soft. She wished she knew whether that meant anything to him.

She longed to look at him, but instead watched the sound, a sheet of silver in the fading light. A fishing boat drew a diagonal line across the water, and a pair of pelicans bobbed and rocked in its wake.

"I see why you love it."

Luke stroked the back of her hand, and she seemed to feel that delicate touch with every cell of her being.

"A person could get lost here and never want to be found," he said.

She should tell him, she thought again.

Later, a little voice seemed to whisper in her ear. *Tell him later, because this precious moment will never come again.*

She was being a coward, but she didn't care. She'd enjoy this evening, and do her best to pretend it never had to end.

Chapter Twelve

They stepped out of the restaurant into what Luke was beginning to recognize as a Southern night, with the air so warm and moist it felt soft against your skin. He stopped in the parking lot for a moment, holding Chloe's hand as his eyes grew accustomed to the dark.

Across the sound, the mainland was a dark silhouette against a paler gray sky. Lights winked on, sparkling in clusters along the horizon.

"It looks like another world, doesn't it."

"Maybe it is." Chloe took a deep breath, as if to inhale the musky sweetness of the air. "Have you made a decision yet about going back?"

Going back—to that other world. The reluctance he felt astonished him. Before they went back—before they even considered it—he had to tell her his decision.

"Chloe, there's something I've been wanting to tell you."

She stiffened, her hand drawing out of his. "I have something to tell you, too. I—"

She stopped, looking beyond him. An instant later he heard the noise, too—running footsteps, heavy breathing, a muffled shout. He spun.

A single slim figure shot around the corner of the nearest building, closely followed by three or four more. Even in the half dark, he recognized the boy. It was Theo, and he was in trouble.

Instinct kicked in almost before conscious thought. "Stay here." He snapped the order to Chloe, then ran across the parking lot, shells crunching under his feet. The sound transmuted in his mind to another that fit the emotion better—to feet pounding on hard pavement, shouts echoing off brick walls and bouncing crazily in the confines of an alley.

He knew the feeling. He didn't need to see the hand grab Theo's T-shirt and pull him around, or the punch that bounced off the boy's shoulder as he dodged. He'd been there. He knew what would happen next, with four of them, all bigger and heavier and meaner than Theo was.

Well, not tonight. Theo didn't have to face this alone. Luke was there.

And so was Chloe. He came to a stop a foot from the boys, assessing the situation. Chloe, breath coming quickly, stopped behind him. Of course she'd ignored his order. Chloe was too gutsy to hang back when someone was in trouble, and she'd go to the wall for her family.

Defuse this before it gets any worse, he ordered himself. His fists clenched, and he seemed to hear the survivor of a hundred street fights jeering in the back of his mind. At some level he was ready for a fight, and sixteen years of civilization threatened to vanish in an instant.

He put his hand on Theo's shoulder, moving next to him, letting his size register on the combatants. Slowly he looked them up and down, using the icy stare that had worked equally well whether cowing would-be brawlers in the boardroom or the back alley.

Three of the four retreated a step. The fourth, the one who'd hit Theo, stood his ground. He wore a look that said his old man owned the earth, and running shoes that had probably cost more than Theo's whole wardrobe.

Luke longed to wipe that cocky expression off the kid's face, but he shoved the urge down. Give everybody a chance to save face, and they might get out of this with no more damage.

He drew Theo a little closer. "Good to see you, Theo." He kept his tone casual. "You and your friends want to join us for coffee?"

Theo straightened, eyes never wavering from the face of the biggest kid. "I will. I reckon these guys are headed for home."

Luke lifted an eyebrow, inviting a response. "That right?"

My-daddy-owns-the-world sneered. "I 'reckon' this geechee better stay on his side of the island—isn't that right, boy?"

Luke's control slipped. This kid was everyone who'd ever looked down on him. The boy didn't know how close to the line he was treading.

Apparently mistaking his silence for cowardice, the kid shoved Theo's shoulder. "I said—"

Luke suddenly discovered his hand fisted in the kid's shirtfront. Rage flamed along his veins. He'd—

"Luke." Chloe's voice was soft but it called him to his senses. He saw the fear in the boy's eyes and held on a moment longer, making sure the kid knew his fear had been seen. Then he released him, smoothing the kid's shirt.

"You know," he said easily, "Theo's people have been here two hundred years or so. I guess that gives him the right to go anywhere he wants."

He let his gaze move from one to another of them. None of them met his eyes, and he knew it was over. "I don't think your parents especially want to bail you out tonight, do you?"

They took that for the dismissal it was. In a moment they'd faded back around the corner.

Time to assess damages. Theo had a bloody nose, and the look that met Luke's eyes was half ashamed, half defiant.

"Hope you didn't mind the interference," he said

as casually as if he asked the boy about school. He heard Chloe's indrawn breath and hoped she wouldn't gush over the kid.

"Of course he doesn't." Her voice was tart, but her hand lingered against her brother's cheek. "Theo doesn't want his daddy to bail him out tonight, either, do you, pest?"

Theo managed a smile. "Guess not."

No, he didn't need to worry that his Chloe would put her foot wrong when it came to helping. He might have been surprised at his reaction to this little encounter, but he wasn't surprised at Chloe. She was true-blue loyal to people she cared about.

Something twisted in his gut. How many people would say that about him?

Chloe decided that her stomach wasn't going to disgrace her. If she let herself think about that moment when she realized Theo was in trouble—her stomach lurched again, and she blanked the picture out of her mind. It had been okay. Luke had been there.

"Well." She decided she could trust her voice. "Guess we'd best get you cleaned up before Momma gets a look at her baby boy."

"In here." Luke jerked his head toward the restaurant. "We could all use a cup of coffee right now."

As soon as they were inside, she saw the blood on Theo's T-shirt. Her stomach tightened all over again.

Luke took her brother's arm and turned him toward the rest room.

"You order the coffee," he said.

Chloe battled down her resentment at his assumption of authority. She hadn't resented it when he'd jumped into Theo's battle, had she? She slid into the nearest booth and ordered coffee for three.

When the waitress had gone, she wrung a napkin between her fingers. If Luke hadn't been there, what would she have done? Well, she'd have helped Theo, of course. But she might have had to yell for help, involved other people, maybe even the police. She shuddered at the thought of the scene.

No, Luke was right. None of them wanted Daddy to bail them out tonight.

The coffee arrived, and she poured a cup for herself without waiting for the other two. Luke had taken control, all right. For a moment she'd actually thought he was going to hit that smart-mouth kid.

She stirred the coffee, starting a dark whirlpool that seemed to match the one in her mind. What had she seen in Luke in those moments? Something wild, something dark, something completely at odds with the sophisticated, urban professional he was the rest of the time. She didn't know where that other person had come from, and she wasn't sure what to make of him.

The rest room door swung, and they came out. Theo's shirt was damp but clean. He shivered a little in the air-conditioning as he slid into the booth, and she shoved a coffee cup toward him.

"Have some. It'll make a new man of you."

The bench creaked as Luke sat next to her. "Some for me, please. I could stand to be a new man."

She glanced sideways at his face. His mouth was a straight, hard line, and some emotion she couldn't guess at darkened his blue eyes. Uncomfortable, she looked at his hands, instead. His strong fingers tore a napkin methodically into strips. He seemed to become aware of that, and he pressed his hands flat against the table.

"I guess I owe you one." Theo stared down at his coffee and grimaced. "Boy, is Daddy gonna say, 'I told you so.'"

"Your daddy doesn't seem like the kind of man to do that."

Luke's voice was calm; the streak of wildness she'd seen vanquished for the moment.

"How'd that get started, anyway?"

Theo shrugged, the movement of thin shoulders under the damp T-shirt bringing a lump to her throat. It seemed like yesterday that she'd been teaching him to ride a bike. Now he was nearly grown.

"It was a girl."

Luke's mouth quirked. "Theo, most of the trouble men end up in starts with the same words. 'It was a girl.'"

Chloe punched his arm, her fist bouncing on hard muscle. "That's right, blame it on Eve."

That brought a smile to Theo's troubled face. "Guess you're right, at that. Anyway, seemed like she liked me. Made them mad. They were waiting when I got off work." His jaw worked. "I should have fought them. Reckon I acted like a coward."

The misery in his voice put a loop around Chloe's heart. What could she say that would make it better? If only Miranda were here. Miranda always knew what to say when someone was hurting. Poor Theo was stuck with the wrong sister tonight.

"Yeah, right. That'd make your daddy proud." Luke's brisk words were like a dash of cold water. "He'd really appreciate your brawling in the street."

Well, it wasn't the dose of sympathy she'd been looking for, but it made Theo sit up a bit straighter.

"I guess that's so." Theo seemed to search Luke's face for answers. "But shouldn't a man defend himself?"

"Looked to me as if you were ready to fight if you didn't have a choice. And there were four of them," Luke reminded him. "There's a difference between being brave and being stupid. That's a line I crossed a time or two myself."

Theo seemed to process that and come to the same conclusion Chloe had. "You knew how to handle yourself out there."

Just what she'd been thinking. Luke had behaved like a man who'd been in that spot more than once.

Luke shrugged. "It didn't take much to scare them off, once they saw they didn't outnumber you."

"Four to two," Theo said.

Chloe ruffled his hair. "Four to three. I didn't grow up running with the twins without learning a thing or two, remember."

Theo grinned. "My sister, the bantam-weight."

"Just one thing bothers me." Luke had a question in his eyes.

"What?"

"What exactly is a geechee? Or is it so bad I shouldn't ask in polite company?"

Laughter bubbled up, dissipating the last of Chloe's tension. "Actually, we consider it a badge of honor. A geechee is anyone born and bred in the low country—roughly speaking, the coast from Georgetown down to the Ogeechee River in Georgia."

"Then, I guess I better get you two geechees home." The ugliness that had marred the evening disappeared entirely as Luke tossed a bill on the table and stood.

Chloe slid out of the booth, feeling his hand close on her elbow. Something, some trace of that other Luke she'd seen tonight, lingered in his touch.

Which was the real Luke? Was she ever going to know?

The inn slept behind her as Chloe stepped out onto the front porch a few hours later. They'd gotten Theo into the house without encountering anyone. Whether or not the boy decided to confide in Daddy was up to him now.

She should have fallen right to sleep from sheer exhaustion. Instead she'd tossed and turned, listening to Miranda's even breathing from the other bed. Finally she'd gotten up and slipped on jeans and a shirt. Maybe a breath of air would counteract the coffee she'd drunk.

The sweet, musky scent of the marshes filled her as she leaned against the porch railing. It always soothed her. It soothed her now. But the question still bubbled beneath the surface. What secrets did Luke hide? How did she reconcile the man she thought she knew with the glimpses he'd given her of his hidden self?

Something moved out on the dock, and a figure was silhouetted against the gray water beyond. Her heart recognized him, even in the dark. *Luke.*

She'd taken three steps off the porch before she'd made a conscious decision to go to him. Well, she had to thank him for what he'd done for Theo tonight, didn't she? But she knew she had another, deeper reason. She had to talk with Luke because she had to know what was going on inside him.

She felt Luke's gaze on her as she crossed the path and stepped onto the dock. The weathered boards echoed hollowly under her feet. He sat at the end, his back against a post.

"Hey." She dropped down next to him.

"Hey, yourself. How's Theo?" His baritone rumble seemed scarcely louder than the murmur of water against the dock.

"Sound asleep." She hesitated, not sure what else to say, her gaze tracing the line of moonlight on the water.

He followed the direction of her gaze. "Beautiful, isn't it. Almost looks like a path."

She smiled. "Gran used to tell us bedtime stories about fishermen who sailed up that path and spent the night throwing their cast nets and pulling in stars. Then we'd go to sleep and dream about it."

"You had a magical childhood, Chloe Elizabeth." His voice had roughened. "Plenty of people would envy you that."

She held her breath as she turned to meet his eyes. "Including you?"

Shush, shush, shush. Three waves caressed the dock before he answered.

"You want to hear my story, Chloe? You wouldn't like it."

The bitterness in his voice startled her, but she wouldn't let it scare her off. They'd come too far for that.

"I want to know whatever you're willing to tell me about yourself." She kept her gaze steady on him, knowing her heart was in her eyes.

He shrugged. "I gave myself away tonight. I knew it. I always knew the street kid was still there. I just didn't realize how close to the surface he was, until

I saw those creeps chasing Theo. I wanted to smash someone.''

His fists clenched as if he felt the urge again. She put her hand on his, feeling the tension that pounded through him. "You didn't."

"I could have." He grasped her wrists suddenly. "Do you really want to know who Luke Hunter is? You want to hear what happens to a kid who never knew a father, whose mother forgot he existed, who was on the streets by the time he was eight? It's not pretty."

His pain wrapped around her heart, hurting her, too. "Who took care of you?"

"Nobody." He spit out the word. "Foster homes for a while, each one worse than the last. I finally figured out that I could get lost on the streets and take care of myself. Live hard, die young—that was my motto."

She wanted to put her arms around him. She wanted to hold him the way she'd have held Theo when he was little and hurting. But his grip on her wrists held her off, and that had to be deliberate. Couldn't he let her in?

Oh, Lord, please. Help me to help him.

"What changed?"

Her soft question seemed to pull him back from whatever blackness he looked into. His grasp eased, as if he became aware that he might be hurting her.

"I met someone." He paused, then continued. "I

walked into the Fresh Start Mission in search of a free meal.''

Things fell into place in her mind. "It was like the Sonshine Center."

He nodded. "Figured I'd find some patsy I could milk for a few bucks. But the Rev was no patsy."

"The Rev?"

"That's what we called him. The Reverend Dr. Thomas Phillips. A Harvard degree, a stint as a military chaplain in Vietnam, and twenty years' worth of scraping kids off the street and pounding some sense into them. He took one look at me and decided he saw something worth saving." A muscle twitched in his jaw. "Can't imagine what."

She stroked his fingers, longing to soothe him and not sure how. "Intelligence. Tenacity. Integrity."

"Is that what you think you see?"

His voice was angry, but she heard the longing underneath the pain. She touched his cheek, her fingertips smoothing the tension away. "That's what I know I see. Whatever you came from, whatever wrong was done to you, that's who you are."

"Chloe, honey, I'm not sure you know what you're saying." His tone was half laughing, half despairing.

She paused for a heartbeat, hearing the soft splash of some night bird after a fish. "This place—since we came, I've begun to see who I am. Maybe that's the magic here. It makes you see who you are. It makes me know I'm not wrong about the man Luke Hunter is, no matter what he came from.''

His hand covered hers, pressing her palm flat against his cheek. His skin warmed to her touch, connecting them at some level she couldn't comprehend.

''I hope you're right. Chloe, I only hope you're right.''

He drew her hand against his lips, and she felt them move in a gentle kiss. Then he pulled her into his arms, and his lips found hers.

Her arms slid around him. They fit together perfectly, as if they were meant to be that way.

Home. She really had come home.

Chapter Thirteen

Why was God confronting him with his past now, when he was on the verge of achieving everything he'd always dreamed he wanted? Luke leaned against the porch railing Monday morning, unable to get the question out of his mind. First the Sonlight Center, then Theo's trouble, reminding him, refusing to let him hide who he was.

He hadn't hidden anything Saturday night when he'd told Chloe things he'd never told anyone, when he'd kissed her and tried to believe they had a future together. The feeling had gained momentum during the service in the tiny chapel on Sunday, continuing to build throughout the family gathering that apparently was a given for the Caldwell clan on Sunday afternoon.

He still didn't have an answer. He'd tried bargaining with God. Hadn't he played fair? Hadn't he sent a monthly check to the Rev to support his mission, even when he couldn't afford it? What more did God want from him?

A white gull swooped down to perch on the dock where he'd sat with Chloe on Saturday night. He'd expected a reaction from her when he told her his past. He hadn't expected warmth, affection, acceptance. *Love.*

His native caution shied away from that word. What did love mean to somebody like him? He'd never known the kind of love Chloe had experienced every moment of her life. How could he possibly hope to give her that?

One thing was certain, through all the doubts that clouded his mind. He had to tell Chloe what he'd decided about Angel Isle. He'd kept that quiet far too long, making excuses for why they were staying when he was actually researching siting the hotel on Angel Isle.

He heard the creak of the screen door and knew it was Chloe even before he turned. She wore her usual shorts and T-shirt, but she exuded a confidence that was new to her. It almost seemed she'd gained all the confidence he'd lost.

"Hey." Her eyes were lit with pleasure. "I have a surprise for you." She crossed the porch to link her arm with his.

"What surprise?" Maybe the surprise was that her most casual touch made him want to kiss her.

"The twins have to go to Savannah today, so I

volunteered us to lead their kayak tour.'' She smiled up at him. ''Since you're turning into such a pro with the kayak, I thought you wouldn't mind.''

''I've only been out twice, remember? That hardly makes me a pro.'' Once he'd have thought the suggestion insane. The fact that now it sounded great only proved how far he'd fallen.

''All you have to do is paddle along with me. We're taking them into the salt marshes, anyway. The worst that can happen if someone topples out is that they'll get their feet muddy. Okay?''

''Okay.'' At some point during this excursion, they'd have the opportunity for a private talk. He'd tell her about his plans and draw her in. He'd make her understand that Angel Isle was the perfect spot for the new hotel, make her see how her family would benefit.

He tried to suppress his misgivings. She'd go along with him. They were a team, weren't they?

Somehow the opportunity for a private talk didn't come as easily as he'd expected. During the ride to the public dock where they were to meet their group, Chloe briefed him about the trip. And once they arrived, the small group of tourists totally occupied her.

He helped unload the kayaks from the truck and watched Chloe slip into her tour guide persona. She gave a quick orientation, handed out life jackets, assigned people to kayaks. He assessed the group. Two older couples, one father and teenage son, one single man with a paunch and a Hawaiian shirt.

Mr. Hawaiian Shirt was the only troublemaker. He didn't want to put on a life jacket.

"I'm sorry, Mr. Carey." Chloe's tone was perfectly polite and perfectly inflexible. "Life jackets are required. If you don't care to wear one, I'll happily refund your money."

Grumbling under his breath, the man yanked on the life jacket. Luke hid a grin when he had to pull it back off to let the straps out. This was going to be an interesting trip.

Chloe finally had them all into the boats and headed down the creek into the marshes.

"Nice guy," Luke commented softly, nodding toward the troublemaker as he matched his stroke to Chloe's.

She flashed him an understanding look over her shoulder. "There's always at least one in every trip—the hotshot businessman who thinks the rules don't apply to him."

"Ouch. That wouldn't include present company, would it?"

Her grin was mischievous. "What do you think?"

Before he could come up with a snappy response, she'd raised her voice so the whole group could hear.

"That's an osprey off to your left, fishing for his dinner. And coming up on the right, you can see several egrets. The salt marsh teems with food for all kinds of shorebirds."

"What about dolphins?" the teenager called out. "Your brochure said we'd see dolphins."

"There's a good chance of that." Chloe rested her paddle across the boat and pulled her ball cap down over her eyes. "They come into the marshes to feed, too."

They paddled past the watching egrets, elegant on their long legs. "You're going to have a disappointed kid if you don't produce dolphins," he said under his breath.

Chloe shrugged. "We can only show them what's here. Trouble is, people don't realize these are wild creatures, not house pets."

A turtle glided past, surprisingly agile in the water, and then a pair of herons made an appearance. The kayaks rounded a curve in the sea of marsh grass, and Chloe raised her hand to stop the procession.

"There," she said, and Luke heard the love in her voice. "Dolphins."

"Wow." The boy let his kayak drift closer to theirs. "What are they doing? Is something wrong with them?"

"It's called strand feeding. Don't get too close, and we'll be able to watch them. They actually throw themselves up on the bank to feed, then slide back into the water."

"Awesome."

Luke knew how the kid felt. Three dolphins threw their bodies in shining arcs out of the water, then slid back in perfect rhythm. It was like watching a ballet.

"No closer, please," Chloe snapped, and Luke tore his gaze from the dolphins.

Predictably it was Carey, paddling toward the dolphins, then juggling his paddle to raise a camera.

"Gotta get a picture of this." Ignoring Chloe, he pushed closer, then lost his paddle with a splash.

Two of the dolphins slid back into the water and disappeared. The third dolphin, apparently startled into losing his rhythm, stranded, floundering helplessly in the mud.

"Get back." Chloe grabbed the paddle as it floated by and tossed it to the man.

"Hey, I paid my money. I've got a right to take a picture."

Luke planted his paddle against the offending kayak and gave it a fierce shove. "Back. Now."

The man swallowed, then let his kayak drift out into the center of the stream. Luke turned to Chloe. "What do we do?"

She watched the dolphin intently, then shook her head. "He's never going to get off there by himself. I'll have to help him." Before he could guess what she was about, she'd slid out of the kayak and was standing waist-deep in the water. "Stay there."

"Not likely." He slid out of the kayak, too, feeling his feet sink ankle-deep into the soft bottom. He shoved their kayak over to the boy. "Hold on to this for me. And don't let anyone get any closer."

The boy nodded, eyes wide.

Chloe moved gently toward the dolphin. Mimicking her movements, Luke closed in on the other side. "Tell me what to do," he whispered.

"We'll have to try and slide him back. He's not going to like being touched." Her eyes never left the dolphin as she eased in next to it.

She reached out slowly, obviously trying to avoid frightening the creature. The instant she touched it, the dolphin went into a frenzy of movement, struggling to get away from her.

Luke closed in on the other side, grabbing for a handhold on the slippery body. The only thing he got for his trouble was a face full of water. He wiped his eyes and looked at Chloe. "Now what?"

"Let me try." She leaned closer, crooning softly. The dolphin's dark, liquid eye seemed to watch her. "There, now, beautiful. We're not going to hurt you. We're just going to get you back into the water, back where you belong. It's all right."

Maybe the creature was too exhausted to fight any longer. Or maybe it heard the love in Chloe's voice. This time when she touched it, there was no struggle.

She slid the dolphin back an inch, then another. Luke had the sense that everyone watching held his breath. She paused, then nodded to Luke. He took hold gingerly, feeling smooth skin throbbing with life.

"Now," Chloe whispered.

They pulled together. The dolphin slid, caught, then slid again into the water. For an instant it simply bobbed on the gentle current. Luke felt it tremble under his hands. Then, with a surge and a ripple that nearly knocked him off his feet, it was gone.

Chloe wiped water from her face. "We did it." Her voice choked a little on the words, and her eyes filled with tears. "We did it."

"You did it."

You're amazing. That was what he wanted to say, but he contented himself with brushing a strand of wet hair off her cheek. They stood waist-deep in the warm water, sharing their triumph, and he felt so close to Chloe that it terrified him.

In a haze of happiness, Chloe loaded the last of the kayaks and said goodbye to the tour group. All she could see was Luke's face as they had watched the dolphin swim free. Surely that had been love in his eyes when he looked at her.

Sunlight glinted on the water, and in the distance she saw the silver crescents of the dolphins working their way toward the sea. They were back where they belonged.

Did she and Luke belong here, together? Her heart seemed to swell at the thought. A few days ago she wouldn't have dared dream of that. Now, anything seemed possible. If a new Dalton Resort did become a reality somewhere in the area, Luke might decide he'd had enough of the pressure cooker that was corporate headquarters. They might—

Luke rounded the truck, a dark shadow with the sun behind him.

She lifted her hand to shield her eyes. "So, what did you think of your first dolphin tour?"

"I hope they're not all that exciting." He nodded toward the departing cars. "Carey's still complaining that I ruined his picture. He's lucky I didn't ruin more than that."

"The customer is always right, remember? You should hear some of the stories the twins tell about the groups they've taken out. It would turn your hair gray."

He smiled, but it was almost mechanical, as if his mind worried away at something else. A chill seemed to settle on her, in spite of the heat of the day.

She tried to tell herself she was imagining things, but it didn't quite work. Something was wrong—she knew Luke too well to be mistaken about that. "Is something wrong?"

"I need to talk with you."

It was his office voice, the voice that gave orders and expected them to be obeyed. She felt herself tighten.

"You want to sign up to lead another tour?" She adjusted the cord on the kayaks, keeping her voice light, trying to hold off whatever was coming.

He moved impatiently, then planted his hand against the truck, leaning close to her. "This is business."

She nodded, trying to assume her office self. But she seemed to have lost that person during the days they'd spent on the island.

"What is it?" Her voice didn't sound natural, even to herself.

"I've made a decision about the site I'm recommending."

He frowned, not looking at her, and that fact sent her tension level soaring. Whatever he'd decided, she wasn't going to like it.

Then his gaze fixed on her, as if to compel her agreement. "I've decided on Angel Isle."

Shock leached the sunlight from the day. "You can't be serious." This was a joke—it had to be.

Luke's frown deepened. "I'm always serious about business, Chloe. If I get the go-ahead from the office, I plan to make your father an offer for the tract of land from the cottage down to the end of the island. Angel Isle is the perfect site. I'm sure you've thought that yourself."

She could only shake her head, as if to shake off his words.

"No, I haven't. You can't." Maybe she should have seen it coming, but it had completely blindsided her.

"Can't?" He lifted his eyebrows in disbelief, probably because subordinates didn't say "can't" to Luke Hunter. "That's why I'm here, remember?"

"I know, I know." Her words tumbled over each other in her rush to make him understand. "But not Angel Isle. You've seen how much it means to us. To me."

That was the crux of it. That was why her heart hurt so much that she pressed her hand against her chest. Luke had to know what Angel Isle meant to her. Yet his decision made one thing very clear. His career was far more important to him than she could ever be.

"I don't understand you, Chloe." Every line of his body spoke of his determination. "Angel Isle is perfect for the new hotel. Your father will find Dalton's offer very appealing, and you can't tell me he doesn't need the money. This could mean a world of difference to your family financially."

Fresh pain clutched her heart. This really was the old Luke speaking, the one who valued money and status above everything. He couldn't see beyond that.

And what about Daddy? If Luke made the kind of offer he was talking about, would her father refuse? Or would he feel compelled to accept whether he wanted to or not, in order to secure his children's futures? None of them would want to sacrifice their right to Angel Isle, no matter how much money was involved. But Daddy might not see it that way.

She could tell her family the truth—that there was no relationship with Luke. That this was all a lie, and Luke had come here for business purposes only. She cringed away from the hurt and disappointment she'd see in their faces.

Please, let there be another way. Please, Lord.

"Luke, please." It was difficult to speak calmly about something so vital. "You have to understand what the island means to us. We can't let it go."

"You wouldn't lose the cottage, Chloe. We can negotiate a deal that leaves it."

"It wouldn't be the same."

His eyes darkened, and he looked at her as if from a great distance. "That's up to your father to decide, isn't it? You told me he owns it."

"Please," she said again, grasping for the words that would open his eyes.

The cleft in his chin seemed chiseled from stone. She put her hand on his arm, and it felt like iron. Why had she ever imagined he was softening toward her? Luke was moving into deal mode. She knew what that meant. If you didn't go along with him, you could expect to be flattened. But she had to try.

"There are plenty of beautiful spots that are much more suitable. I've shown you a dozen or more."

"Nothing as good as Angel Isle."

"But without a bridge, every guest would have to be ferried across to the island. That's got to add to the difficulty."

"And to the appeal," he shot back. "People like the idea of getting away from everything to a deserted isle."

Her deserted isle. But that was a selfish way of looking at it. She had to concentrate instead on all the future generations of Caldwells who wouldn't have the island as a haven if this deal went through.

She tightened her grasp on his arm, looking into his eyes. "Just do this for me. Give me a few days to find a site that will work as well. Please."

She held her breath while Luke stared at her,

frowning. The seconds ticked away, punctuated by the cry of a gull. It sounded as desolate as she felt.

Finally he nodded. "All right, Chloe. If it means that much to you, I'll take a little more time. But I don't understand."

He didn't understand. The dreams she'd harbored about their future dissolved like the ebbing tide spreading out on the sand. He didn't understand, and he never would. If she'd been looking for something to illustrate the differences between them, she couldn't have come up with anything clearer than this.

He'd been landed back in the real world with a painful *thump*. Luke snapped his cell phone closed and stalked to the window of his sunlit bedroom at the inn. Two hours ago, he'd told Chloe he'd give her time to find another site for the hotel. Now he didn't have any time to give.

The sound of Dalton's voice had been enough to remind him where he belonged. And Dalton's message had been perfectly clear. He wasn't interested in waiting. He didn't want to consider other possibilities. Everything was a go on the Angel Isle site; wrap it up before the locals get wind of it and prices soar. The implication was clear. If Luke couldn't close this, he wasn't vice-presidential material.

Luke stared at the small boat nosing idly into the dock. A gull swooped down and perched on its rail, looking as if it welcomed the boat home.

Fantasy. Everything about this place had the air of a fantasy. It wasn't for him. His world was back in Chicago, at corporate headquarters. He belonged there, in a plush new corner office.

And Chloe? Where did she belong?

The question came, unbidden. Even back in Chicago, Chloe had been somehow a little different. She'd always seemed to belong somewhere else.

His jaw clenched. The thought reminded him uncomfortably of the Rev's favorite sermon topic. *Always remember that this world isn't really your home. God designed you to live forever with Him.*

He'd been thinking far too much about the Rev and the mission since he'd been on the island. The mission had been its own little world, too. Maybe that was why.

Not my world, he told himself again. The future he'd envisioned all his life hinged on this deal, and he wouldn't let it slip away.

Determination hardened inside him. He'd find Chloe, he'd tell her what he had to do, and he'd wind up the deal. In a month, these days and nights on Caldwell Island would be just a memory.

He walked quickly out of the room and down the steps, fueled by determination. See Chloe, make her understand. Then he'd approach her father.

But Chloe was nowhere to be found. And when Luke stepped out onto the porch in search of her, Clayton Caldwell was coming up the steps, limping a little.

"Luke." Clayton greeted him with considerably less suspicion than he had that first day. "How did the kayak trip go? You lose any tourists?"

"No, we brought them all back. But there was one I wouldn't have minded losing."

Clayton smiled. "Guess there always is." His smile faded. "I've been wanting to thank you. My boy told me what happened Saturday night. I'm grateful to you."

"It was nothing." Luke tried to shrug it off. "Lucky I was there, or Chloe might have started a riot. I'm glad Theo told you about it. He's a good kid."

"Guess he's not such a kid as I thought. He went right back to the club the next day, faced down those boys. Told me a man doesn't run away from trouble."

Luke's own words echoed back at him. "So he's okay?"

Clayton nodded. "Even got a date for Saturday night out of it." The lines in his face deepened, and Luke knew he was thinking about his own experience. "Guess maybe attitudes have changed a little, at least."

Clayton put his hand on Luke's shoulder, as he might with one of his own sons. "Anyway, I'm grateful to you," he said, with such gravity that he might be making a solemn oath.

Luke cleared his throat. "You know, there's something I've been wanting to talk to you about."

"No time like the present." Clayton leaned against the porch rail.

Chloe would think *any* other time better, but Chloe wasn't here. And he had to get this wound up before his goal slipped from his grasp.

"Chloe and I were talking about the land you own on Angel Isle. I'm interested in making a deal for a piece of it. I—"

Clayton shoved himself away from the railing, beaming. "Is that what's been on your mind? Boy, why didn't you tell me that before?"

The response startled him. "Chloe thought I should wait."

"No point in waiting, when a man knows what he wants."

"There'll have to be a survey. We'll look at the market value, of course."

Chloe's father thrust out his hand. "We'll do what's fair. We both know that. My hand is my bond."

Luke took his hand. Either he was dreaming, or this was the easiest negotiation he'd ever done. "I appreciate your confidence. Now, about the details—"

"Luke!"

He turned. Chloe stood in the doorway, eyes wide with shock and hurt.

Chapter Fourteen

"Luke." Chloe pressed her hand against the door frame. The worn wooden edge felt real. It was the only thing that did. "What's going on?"

Say something, she demanded silently. *Tell me that what I think is happening isn't. Tell me I'm wrong, and that you didn't just betray me.*

Her father smiled. "Luke and I came to an arrangement, sugar. He's buying a tract of land on Angel Isle." He glanced at Luke. "Am I talkin' out of turn? You didn't say it was meant to be a secret."

"No, it's not a secret." Luke's voice flattened, giving nothing away. "Chloe knows about it."

"I know that you promised me you'd wait." She had to fight to keep the pain from her voice, and she probably wasn't succeeding, because it throbbed along her veins and choked her throat. "You agreed to give me time to find an alternative site."

His face froze into his competitive mask—edgy, determined. "The situation has changed."

"What has changed?" She pushed herself away from the door and stalked toward them, trying to concentrate on her anger so she wouldn't feel the pain. "What could possibly justify breaking your word to me?"

His jaw was clenched so hard it looked as if it might break. "This is business, Chloe. You know that. Mr. Dalton called. He wants the deal completed at once. I didn't have the luxury of waiting for you to be ready."

That business arrogance of his—she'd seen it turned against other people. She'd never expected to see it turned against her.

"Dalton?" Her father looked from her to Luke. "Who's Dalton?"

"The head of Dalton Resorts," Chloe said before Luke could answer. "The company we work for."

"What's he got to do with Luke buying land so he can build a home for the two of you?"

She had thought she couldn't hurt any worse than she already did, but this stabbed her in the heart. Daddy thought Luke wanted a home with her. A *life* with her. That was why he'd agreed. This had happened because she'd lied to the people who mattered most in the world to her.

"You misunderstood." To do him justice, Luke looked as appalled as she felt. "I wasn't making the offer for myself, Mr. Caldwell. I was making it for

Dalton Resorts. We want to build a hotel on Angel Isle.''

"A hotel,'' her father echoed. He frowned at her. "Chloe, does any of this make sense to you?''

"Daddy—'' She went to him then, clutching his hands in hers, trying to convey her regret through her touch. "I'm sorry. This shouldn't have happened. None of this should have happened.'' Shame burned deep inside. *I'm sorry, I'm so sorry. Forgive me.*

"Chloe, you don't have to say anything.'' Luke frowned at her, and his message was clear. She didn't have to expose the charade she'd carried out.

But he was wrong. She did have to.

She took a deep breath, wondering how her heart could keep on beating when it hurt so much. "Daddy, this has all been a lie. Luke and I have never been involved with each other. We're not a couple.''

Her father shook his head slowly, as if her words didn't make any sense. "Then, why did he come here?''

"I wanted to check out the area for a new Dalton Resort,'' Luke said, apparently determined not to let her speak for him. "I'm sorry about the confusion, but that's all I'm interested in.''

All he was interested in. Chloe bit down hard on her lip and tried not to think about those words.

Her father didn't look at Luke, only at her. "Chloe? Child, why did you do this?''

There weren't any reasons good enough. "I'm

sorry, Daddy.'' She blinked back hot tears. ''Gran thought we were dating, and she invited him to her birthday. And he—''

''It was business,'' Luke said. ''Just business. I asked Chloe to play along, to give me an excuse for being here.''

He probably thought he was helping, but he wasn't. Her father didn't so much as glance at Luke. He just stared searchingly into her eyes, and she felt very small and very ashamed.

''I'm sorry,'' she whispered again. ''I shouldn't have let it go this far.''

''No.'' Her father's level gaze told her just how disappointed in her he was. ''No, you shouldn't have.''

She tried to wrap her mind around a way to make things right. ''At least you don't have to go through with this. You don't have to sell.''

He straightened. ''I gave my hand, child, and I don't back down when I've given my hand.'' He looked at Luke then, and his expression was almost pitying. ''You'll tell me when you have the papers ready.''

Without waiting for an answer, he turned and disappeared into the house.

Luke tried not to let the relief he felt show on his face. For a moment he'd seen the whole deal dissolving, seen his future at Dalton dissolving right along with it. Dalton wouldn't easily have forgiven his spending this much time and coming back empty-handed.

The deal was safe, but Chloe still had to be placated. "Chloe, I'm sorry."

"You're not sorry." The face she turned on him was the face of a stranger. "Why should you be? You're getting what you want."

"I'm sorry for the way it happened. Sorry that it all came out that way. I certainly didn't plan that. But Dalton put pressure on me to wrap this up quickly."

"So you put pressure on my father."

He'd never known her golden-brown eyes could look so scornful. He beat down the little voice that said she had every right.

"I didn't pressure him. I just opened the subject, and he agreed before I had a chance to give him the details."

"He didn't understand." She threw the words at him. "Thanks to our playacting, he agreed to something he never would have otherwise."

"You don't know that. When he heard what Dalton is willing to pay, he'd have jumped at it, anyway." He would, of course he would. Anyone would.

"If you really believe that, let him off the hook." Her words challenged him. "Start all over again and make your offer."

She was asking the impossible. "Chloe, I can't do that, not now. You must realize that. Dalton wouldn't forgive me if I let the deal slip between my fingers at this point."

"And that's all that matters to you."

She was judging him again. He embraced anger. She had no right to judge him. She didn't. No one did.

"I'm doing what I was hired to do. If you don't understand that, maybe you don't belong at Dalton Resorts."

The instant the words were out of his mouth, he was appalled. He didn't want to lose Chloe. He didn't want to think about returning to Chicago without her.

But the alternative seemed to be losing his dream, and he couldn't do that, either. He couldn't give up the goal that had sustained him all these years.

Chloe went white but her gaze never wavered. "Maybe you're right about that. Maybe I don't belong there, any more than you belong here."

There didn't seem to be anything left to say.

"I'll pack my things." He moved past her to the door. "It will be better if I move to a hotel on the mainland."

She stepped aside, as if touching him might contaminate her. "Yes. That will be better."

He yanked open the screen door. "Please tell your father I'll call him to arrange a meeting with an attorney to sign the papers."

Something inside cried to him to say something else, to mend this with Chloe no matter what the cost.

He slammed it down hard. He couldn't change now, not when he was on the verge of having everything he wanted.

Then, why did that seem so hollow?

By evening, her family's sympathy had become intolerable. Chloe huddled in a rocker on the porch, feet pulled up, arms wrapped around her knees. If she'd ever doubted their love, she couldn't doubt it now. The knowledge of her deception had rocked them. They had to be disappointed in her. But one and all, they'd rallied around.

Daniel had suggested taking Luke for a nice long boat ride and marooning him. David wanted to call an attorney. Miranda thought if they just explained how they felt, surely Luke would understand. Theo had been at first disbelieving, then furious. His idol had shown his feet of clay, and Theo wasn't going to find that easy to forgive.

The bottom line, though, was that Daddy wouldn't change his mind. Whatever it cost him, his path was clear. He'd given his word.

It was her fault. Chloe leaned her forehead on her knees. When she was six and had done something wrong, she'd curled up in a ball in the futile hope that she could just disappear. It hadn't worked then, and it didn't work now.

They were going to lose Angel Isle, and it was all her fault.

Daniel's truck pulled into the drive. A door

slammed, and Gran marched toward her. The family had called in the big guns, she thought tiredly. But Gran was just someone else to whom she owed an apology.

"Gran, I'm sorry." She wouldn't have thought she had any tears left to shed, but they welled in her eyes. "I deceived you. I'm so sorry."

Gran just stood for a moment, hands folded on the front of her flower-print dress. "You are a pretty sorry sight, Chloe Elizabeth."

Chloe planted her feet on the floor and wiped her eyes with the back of her hand. "Yes, ma'am."

"As for deceiving me—" Gran sat down in the rocker next to her "—looks to me like the person you most deceived was yourself."

Gran had an uncanny knack for getting right to the thing you least wanted to talk about.

"I guess that's true," she admitted. "I cared about Luke. I kidded myself into believing he cared about me. But he doesn't. He just cares about getting where he's always wanted to be."

"That's him. What about you?"

The question jerked her head up. "What do you mean?"

"I mean *you*, Chloe Elizabeth Caldwell. Why are you sitting here feeling sorry for yourself? Why aren't you doing something about this?"

It was like a cold wave in her face. For a moment she just stared at Gran, and then she managed a smile. "That's what I love about you, Gran. You get right to the point."

Gran sniffed. "No sense my reminding you I love you, is there? You already know that. What about this young man of yours? You love him?"

"I do." She took a shaky breath. "It seems like a pretty stupid move right now, but I do."

"Why?"

The abrupt question took her aback. "Well, I..." *I just do* wasn't a good enough answer. Gran wanted specifics. "Because he's not really like this. At least, I don't think he is, down inside. But he had a terrible life when he was young. He came up from nothing, and he had to fight for everything. He thinks getting this vice-presidency will prove he's arrived. That's been his goal for so long that he can't see past it."

Gran gave a short nod. "'Bout what I figured. He's lost, that's what."

"Lost?" It was a new idea, and she considered it. "I guess you could look at it that way." Although Luke certainly didn't think he was lost.

"It's the truth." Her expression softened. "Like you, Chloe-girl. Our Chloe was lost for a while. But then Luke brought you back, and you started to see what God wants for you, didn't you?"

For a moment, she'd thought what God wanted for her was a life with Luke. But she understood what Gran meant. If she hadn't come back to the island with Luke, she might never have looked at what God's will for her life was. She might never have seen that just having a job and a salary wasn't enough. She had to contribute—had to be needed.

"I guess so, but Luke isn't like me. I'm not even sure what he believes. He had faith once, but it seems like it got buried under all his ambition."

"Lost," Gran said again with certainty. "He's lost, and you've got to rescue him."

"Me? Gran, he's not going to listen to me." *He doesn't care,* her heart cried.

"Chloe Elizabeth, you hear me now." Gran looked at her sternly. "If he were drowning out there in the surf, you'd risk your life to save him, wouldn't you?"

Like the first Chloe. "Yes, but—"

"No 'buts' about it. That young man of yours is drowning, and he doesn't even know it—wanting things and success more than God's plans for him. It's up to you to straighten him out, you heah?"

There was only one answer Gran expected when she asked that. "Yes, ma'am. But it's not going to be easy."

"If it was easy, anybody could do it. It wouldn't take Chloe Elizabeth Caldwell."

Gran clasped her hand firmly, then stood up. "Now I got to talk to that son of mine. Make sure he's doing this because he thinks it's right, not just because he knows it's the opposite of what his brother would do."

Chloe just stared after her. That would never have occurred to her, but obviously Gran was considerably wiser. She knew more about people than Chloe would learn in a lifetime.

And Gran thought Chloe could do this thing.

Chloe forced herself to look at the possibility. How could she make Luke see he was wrong?

One thing was certain. She wouldn't make the mistake again of trying to create a plan without taking it to the Lord. She closed her eyes, seeking the quiet place in her soul that she would feel in the chapel or on Angel Isle. Listening.

A few minutes later she opened her eyes and found she was looking at the *Spyhop*, rocking gently at the dock. Angel Isle. The boat.

An idea began to form in her mind. *Is this it, Lord? Is this what I should be doing?*

A quiet sureness filled her soul. She knew what she had to do. She had to confront Luke with who he was, and she knew just where to do it.

Whether he'd listen to her or not—well, that was up to him. She knew what God expected her to do, and that was enough.

Chapter Fifteen

Luke stood at the public dock in Caldwell Cove the next day, wondering if anything could be more futile than this effort. Why had he come? His meeting in the local attorney's office to sign the preliminary agreements was set for less than three hours away. He wouldn't believe he'd actually pulled this off until he had the agreements in hand.

So why was he here?

He didn't have to search hard for the answer. He knew why. Chloe had called him, Chloe had wanted to see him. And even though he didn't think it would do any good, he had to see her again.

Chloe's face filled his mind, her green eyes dancing, her golden-brown hair curling against sun-kissed skin, her generous mouth smiling at him. He tried to push it away, to replace it with an image of the corner office that would soon be his. The task was more difficult than it should be.

All right, he could deal with this. He'd spent his life setting goals and letting nothing keep him from achieving them. He didn't intend to change now.

The only reason Chloe intruded on his plans was that he didn't like the breach between them. He cared about her, not just as his valued right hand but as...

What? His mind stalled on that. He knew how to think of Chloe as his assistant. He wasn't sure he knew how to relate to her as anything else. But things had changed since they'd come to the island, he couldn't deny that.

He wanted to mend things with her. That much was clear in his mind. Whether or not there could be anything else between them—he just didn't know.

He saw her face again—eyes filled with a sense of betrayal—and something clamped around his heart. Then he looked up and saw the *Spyhop* nosing into the dock with Chloe at the wheel.

She tossed the rope to him, and he caught it automatically. His mind seemed empty of the words he wanted to say. He just looked at her, noting the dark smudges under her eyes and the determined set to her soft mouth.

"Are you all right?" That wasn't what he'd intended to say, but his heart took over.

She shrugged, unsmiling. "I've been better." She gestured to the boat. "Hop in. Let's go for a ride."

"Can't we just talk here?" He glanced at his watch.

"You have plenty of time before your meeting." Her voice was edgy. "Get on board. I want to make one last trip to Angel Isle before your meeting."

"Chloe, I don't think that's a good idea. Look, let's go get a cup of coffee and talk."

She shook her head stubbornly. "Angel Isle." She met his gaze evenly. "I think you owe me that."

Angel Isle was the last place he wanted to go today. But there was a determination about Chloe that was new to her, as if she'd done some growing up overnight. She wasn't the team player, ready to go along with anything he wanted. If he wanted to talk to her, he'd have to do it her way.

"All right." He stepped lightly into the boat. "If it means that much to you."

She didn't answer—just backed away from the dock so quickly he nearly fell into his seat. He clutched the railing with one hand and watched as she turned her face into the wind and the nose of the boat into the channel.

She wasn't looking at him. Eyes narrowed, she stared straight ahead.

"Chloe, look, we have to talk."

She shook her head, gesturing toward her ears. "Can't hear well enough here. Wait until we get to the island."

"We've talked before on the boat. Why not now?"

She swung the boat in a wide semicircle around the end of the island. "You're in a hurry to get to your meeting, remember?" She revved the motor. "So let's just get there."

They passed the yacht club dock, and he wondered if Theo was working today. With a pang, he realized the kid who'd looked at him with so much admiration the other night probably wouldn't speak to him now.

Then Chloe turned the boat into Dolphin Sound, accelerating so that they rocketed across the waves. He clung grimly to the rail and wondered if she was trying to make him seasick. No looking for dolphins today—all he could do was hang on.

Finally she eased in to the dock on Angel Isle, and he took a deep breath and waited for his stomach to catch up with him.

"Trying to make me remember I'm a landlubber?" he asked, climbing onto the dock and making the ropes fast. He wouldn't admit how much he wanted to feel firm ground under his feet.

Chloe scrambled up beside him. "Just wanted you to have a taste of what the sound will be like once there's a resort on Angel Isle—hotel launches rushing back and forth, pleasure boats crowding the water."

She pointed, and he saw the dolphins then, their crescent shapes moving through the waves. Funny, he almost felt he could identify them, the way Sammy had that first day.

"Say goodbye." Chloe's tone was grim. "I don't imagine they'll hang around once the sound becomes jammed."

He ought to be able to find something to say to that, but he couldn't. *It's not my fault.* That was what he wanted to say. "Look, we both know the hotel will bring prosperity. People will be glad we did it. The dolphins will adapt."

She just looked at him. Suddenly he was back waist-deep in the warm water of the marsh, looking at the triumph in Chloe's face as the dolphin shuddered between them and then took off for the sea.

He blinked, shaking his head, shaking away the image. But looking at Chloe today proved just as disturbing. The gold dolphin necklace he'd given her lay against her skin. For an instant his fingertips tingled, as if he were fastening the clasp against the delicate arch of her nape.

He took a step back from her, and the dock moved gently under his feet. "Let's take a walk," he said abruptly. Maybe he'd be able to think more clearly if he wasn't looking at her.

She nodded, and he followed her off the dock and down to the stretch of beach. They fell into step with each other on the hard-packed sand. He frowned, trying to come up with the words that would make things right between them. It shouldn't be this difficult to make peace with Chloe. He'd handled far more costly negotiations than this, without this terrifying sense that the wrong word would ruin everything.

"They won't, you know." Chloe glanced out at the water.

"Who won't?"

"The dolphins. They won't adapt."

"Chloe—" He stopped, again gripped by that fear of saying the wrong thing. "You know you can't stop progress. It's going to come whether you want it or not."

Her glance flashed to him. "Not stop it, no. But progress doesn't have to take away our island."

"Look, I know you love it here." *I feel closer to God on Angel Isle than anyplace else on earth.* That gave him pause. "But are you sure you're not being a little selfish? Don't other people have the right to share the beauty?"

The shadow in her eyes told him the shot had hit home.

"The place as we know it won't exist in ten years if the hotel goes in. That's what you don't understand. Angel Isle is too fragile. Other places can stand up to it, but not Angel Isle."

He'd agreed to let her help him find an alternative site, and then he'd gone back on his word. He'd had a good reason for that, hadn't he?

"Dalton didn't give me a choice." That sounded defensive even to him.

"You always have a choice, Luke. It just depends how big a price you're willing to pay."

They seemed to have cut through all the external arguments. It was as if they spoke to each other's hearts.

"You don't know what you're asking me." He stopped, swinging to face her.

She met his eyes. "I might be the one person who does know."

He knew, suddenly, what he was seeing in her eyes. Love. For him. It crashed over him like a wave, knocking him off his feet.

"Chloe." He took her hands, feeling her pulse beating rapidly against his fingers. "Chloe, I want—"

What did he want? What was he willing to give up to have her? Everything?

He drew her slowly toward him. This was bigger than ambition, bigger than the corner office. This was everything he'd ever wanted. "Chloe." He said her name again softly as she moved into his arms—

The sound ripped through the stillness. He spun.

The *Spyhop's* engine roared, and the boat shot away from the dock toward the open sound with Theo at the wheel.

The meeting—without the boat, he'd never make the meeting. Chloe had invited him here. Chloe had betrayed him.

Chloe stared blankly after the *Spyhop*. "Theo!" she shouted, even knowing how impossible it was for him to hear her. "What does that boy think he's doing?"

She swung to Luke, as if he might have an answer, and then she saw his face. He thought she had done this.

"Luke, I didn't." Tears stung her eyes. Why now, of all times? Surely she'd been getting through to Luke. He'd looked at her as if...as if he loved her.

He didn't look that way now.

"Congratulations, Chloe." His fists clenched. "That was a move worthy of Dalton himself."

"You can't believe I had anything to do with that. Theo's come up with some crazy plan on his own." Probably because Theo had been hurt to discover Luke wasn't the hero he'd thought.

"I'm afraid that's giving your little brother a bit too much credit." He looked at his watch, and his blue eyes darkened with fury. "Perfect timing. I miss the meeting, your father assumes I've backed out, and the deal is off."

"I didn't." She said it again, helpless against his anger. He'd never believe her.

"On the other hand, maybe not such terrific timing." His expression was wry. "Because I was about to give in. About to give up everything for you, because...I thought we were in love."

I thought we were in love. She did feel her heart break then, she was sure of it.

"What happened to that loyalty of yours, Chloe?

It seems to be a pretty flexible commodity these days.''

Anger welled up suddenly, and she welcomed it. If she held on to the anger, maybe she could withstand the pain for a bit.

''Loyalty? You're a fine one to talk about loyalty. About love.'' She had to fight a fresh wave of pain before she could go on. ''Don't even talk about changing for me. You should be making this decision because it's right, not because of me.''

She had lost him. No, that wasn't right. She couldn't lose what she'd never had. But she could still grieve for what might have been.

''What's right is doing the job I came here to do. The job you were supposed to help me do.''

''What's right doesn't have anything to do with business.'' Her head throbbed with the need to make him see.

Oh, Lord, let me get through to him.

''You talked about Reverend Tom and what he meant to you. How he led you to the Lord. Do you actually remember any of that? Do you ever think about doing anything because it's God's will for your life, instead of what you want?''

He went pale. ''Don't preach to me, Chloe. You don't have the right.''

''I love you.'' The words she thought she'd never speak had a bitter taste. ''I think that gives me the right.'' Before he could say anything, she swept on. ''You asked me where my loyalty was. I can tell you that. It's to the man I've always thought you were, inside. But if you go through with this, you're not that man.''

No use, it was no use. He wasn't hearing her. She spun on her heel.

''Where are you going?''

''Theo had to have come by boat.'' She flung the words over her shoulder at him. ''I'm going to find it. If you expect to make that meeting, you'd better hurry.''

Without waiting to see if he was following, she jogged down the sand. She had a pretty good idea where Theo would have beached his boat—same place he'd beached it when he'd run away. And if she concentrated on that and kept moving, maybe she could run away from the pain that threatened to overwhelm her.

Sure enough, Theo's boat was pulled up under a sweep of Spanish moss not more than twenty feet from the dock. She tugged it toward the water.

''We're going across the sound in that?''

''It's the only way.'' She resisted the impulse to imply it wasn't safe. Her father had raised her to act honorably. She wouldn't disappoint him again. ''Theo does it all the time.''

''All right.'' Luke's jaw set. ''Let's do it.'' He grabbed the boat and dragged it to the water.

Of course he'd do it. Chloe shoved them out into deep water. The word *can't* wasn't in Luke's vocabulary. He'd sacrifice anything for the rewards this deal would bring. Anything.

She saw the flash of a dolphin out in the sound, and closed her eyes for a second against her agony.

Gran had been wrong. She wasn't like the first Chloe. She didn't have the strength to save the man she loved.

Chapter Sixteen

He was doing what he had to do. Luke repeated the words to himself as the small boat chugged up to the dock in Caldwell Cove. *What he had to do.* Even Chloe must recognize that. She hadn't spoken to him all the way across the sound.

Just as well. He was furious at the thought of her betrayal. He should be used to that. It was business. But not Chloe. Chloe didn't do things like that.

She eased the boat into the dock, and he looped the rope around the piling and made it tight. Quickly he climbed out, brushing at the water stains on his slacks.

It wasn't the way he'd choose to appear at an important meeting, but it would have to do.

Do you ever think about what God wants you to do? Chloe's voice echoed in his mind, and he blocked it out.

He turned to her. "I assume you're going to the attorney's office, too. You may as well ride with me."

Her mouth pressed into a thin line, and she shook her head. "I'll walk."

A spurt of anger surprised him. "Don't be ridiculous. You've just spent two hours with me. Another five minutes isn't going to compromise you."

For an instant she just stared at him, and he couldn't read her usually expressive face. Then she jerked a nod and stalked to the car.

He followed, unable to reject the thought that swept through him. He cared about those five minutes. He cared because they could be the last ones he'd ever spend in her company. After today, he'd probably never see her again.

Against his will, he took a quick sideways glance at her as she slid into the seat next to him. *He'd never see her again.* It was like having a piece of himself cut away. Chloe knew him better than anyone else in his life.

And he knew *her* better. The thought stuck. He knew Chloe bone deep. He knew what she could do, and what she couldn't. And she couldn't have connived to strand him on Angel Isle so he'd miss the meeting. She couldn't. His certainty shocked him.

He was still grappling with it when he pulled up in front of the office of Caldwell Cove's only attorney. Chloe jumped out as if she couldn't bear to be in his company any longer.

But he was out and around the car before she could reach the door. "Chloe, wait."

He grasped her arm, and it was like grasping a live wire. He felt the shock right to his heart. He released her as she swung toward him.

"What I said before—about you plotting with Theo to maroon me on the island." This was incredibly awkward to say with her looking at him as if he were an insect. "If you didn't, I'm sorry for what I said."

She just continued to stare at him, and he realized he'd been wrong about her look. She wasn't looking at him as if he were an insect. She was looking at him as if he had a repugnant and possibly contagious illness.

"It really doesn't matter now, does it." She turned and walked into the office.

He followed, feeling emptier than he had in a long time. She was right. It didn't matter.

Preston James was a fussy, probably inefficient elderly man who'd obviously known the Caldwell family forever. Luke was prepared to find him trouble to deal with, but the paperwork had been drawn up as he'd requested. Ten more minutes and this would all be over.

James gestured them to seats around a long mahogany table that looked as if it belonged in someone's dining room. Chloe, her parents, the twins and

Miranda lined up in the chairs on one side. Luke took his place across from them, alone.

"Well, I guess we all know why we're here." James put documents in front of Luke and Clayton. "Take one more look at this, please." His comment seemed to be directed more at Clayton than at Luke.

Chloe's mother put her hand on her husband's. His children seemed to draw closer to him. They might not agree with what he was doing, but they were there to support him. They'd stand by him, no matter what happened.

The attorney put down a pen in front of Luke, and it clicked against the table, the only sound in the office. No, not the only sound. Luke could hear his own heart beating. A wave of panic swept over him, like a riptide pulling him to the bottom of the ocean.

When was the last time you asked God what He wanted from you?

Images flickered through his mind, so quickly he could barely identify them, as if he were drowning and his life was passing before his eyes—the Rev, beaming with pride when Luke's college scholarship came through; the day he'd received his MBA, with no one there to help him celebrate; his first office, barely bigger than a broom closet.

His pulse pounded in his ears. Was he having a heart attack? He tried to focus on the document, but other pictures blocked it out. Chloe—hugging her grandmother, frowning over her brother's misdeeds, saving the dolphin. Chloe, looking at him with all

her generous heart in her gaze, saying she loved the
man she thought he was, inside.

What do You want from me, God?

The question he'd avoided all his life thundered in
his mind, ripped from his very soul.

What do You want from me?

He was vaguely aware of the lawyer saying something, vaguely realized the others were looking at
him strangely.

"Are you ready to sign, Mr. Hunter?" The man
held the pen out to him.

The answer he'd tried to escape pooled in his
mind, crystal clear.

"No." He stood, scraping his chair back. He
looked at Clayton. "The offer is withdrawn."

He turned and walked out.

Chloe stood on the dock alone, watching the sun-
set paint the sky with pink and purple. Alone. She'd
struggled through the rest of this unbelievable day,
trying to get her loving family to leave her alone.

After they'd finished wondering and exclaiming
and praising God for the unexpected turn of events
in the lawyer's office, the advice had begun. *Go after
him, Chloe.* That was the gist of it. *Go after him. He
did the right thing, in the end, so go after him.*

She couldn't, not now. Her heart ached. Luke was
fighting it out with Dalton, and more importantly
with God. This part he had to do alone. The only

thing she could do now was pray, and she'd been doing that with all her strength for the past hour.

You showed me the truth about myself, Lord. Please be with Luke. Show him the person he was meant to be.... And bring him back to me. I don't want this to be a selfish prayer, Lord. But bring him back to me.

She heard a step on the dock. When she turned, Luke was there.

For a moment he just stood, looking at her. She met his eyes, half afraid of what she might find there.

Relief swept through her. Peace. That was what she saw at last in his eyes. Peace.

"You came back." She couldn't seem to find any other words. "You came back."

He nodded, stepping closer. But not touching her. "I had some things to take care of." He grimaced. "With Dalton Resorts."

"What happened?" Dalton wouldn't have taken it well, she knew that. She knew exactly what Luke had risked by his actions—the vice-presidency, the future he'd planned for himself.

"Let's just say I'm not in the running for vice-president any longer."

"I'm sorry."

"I'm not." He shrugged. "Funny, I never thought I'd say that, but I'm not. Anyway, I finally talked Dalton into considering another site in the area. I'll be staying long enough to find it. Then—well, I've had a lot of thinking to do today about where my life goes next. You know, don't you?''

''Wrestling with God. That's what Gran calls it. Wrestling with God.''

''Exactly.'' His face looked relaxed, almost younger. ''I'd managed to avoid that all my life, and all of a sudden, thanks to you, I couldn't anymore.''

The last bit of fear she'd been holding onto vanished. Whatever happened between them, Luke had found his way back to his Father. ''Not me,'' she said. ''You did this on your own.''

''Only because you made me face it. 'Have you asked what God wants of your life?' That's what you said. That's what wouldn't let me go.''

Gran had said Chloe would have to rescue him, and Chloe had thought she couldn't—known she couldn't in her own strength. But she hadn't done it alone.

''If I said the right words, it was because God gave them to me.''

Luke reached out then, touching her cheek gently. ''I know. God made a lot of things clear to me, once I started listening—'' His voice broke suddenly, and he cleared his throat. ''I looked at your father, willing to sacrifice something he loved for the sake of honor. And I knew that's the kind of man God wants me to be.''

Her heart was so full she couldn't speak, and tears filled her eyes. She let them spill over onto her cheeks, and Luke wiped them away, his fingertips warm on her skin.

"That's the man I've always seen, inside," she whispered. "An honorable man. The man I love."

Luke spread his hands wide, empty. "This is all I have to offer, Chloe. Just myself, and an uncertain future. Will you have me?"

She stepped into his outstretched arms and felt them close around her.

"That's all I ever wanted," she said, heart overflowing with love and gratitude. "Just you."

Epilogue

~

Two months later

"Come away from that door, Chloe Elizabeth Caldwell. Do you want the groom to see you before the ceremony?"

Gran closed the door into the sanctuary, but not before Chloe had seen St. Andrew's filled to capacity with family and friends. They'd cheerfully overflowed to the groom's side, taking the place of the family Luke didn't have.

Even Cousin Matt was there, all the way from Indonesia this time. The faintest shadow clouded her happiness. Something was wrong with Matt. She'd sensed it, and so had Gran. Something aside from the wedding had brought him home.

Keep him in Your hands, Lord. Let him find what he seeks here on Caldwell Island.

"It's all right, Gran." Chloe squeezed her grandmother's hand. "Theo's keeping Luke safely out of sight." Theo, having been struck dumb by Luke asking him to be the best man, had recovered to a determination to be the best best man anyone had ever seen.

Miranda, her long skirt flowing about her, knelt to adjust the folds of cream silk around Chloe's ankles, and her mother fastened the last button on the long sleeves of the dress she'd worn for her own wedding.

"Perfect," she said, smiling through a sheen of tears. "Just perfect."

Perfect, Chloe echoed silently. How could it not be perfect, when she was marrying the only man she'd ever love, the man God had chosen for her.

The door opened, and Sammy popped his head in. "The Rev says they're ready when you are."

Miranda frowned at him, ready to correct him for using Luke's nickname for Reverend Tom, but Chloe shook her head. Reverend Tom had become part of the family in the few days since he'd arrived to assist with the ceremony. Chloe had been prepared to love him on sight, and she had.

It was thanks to his wise counsel that Luke had taken a job with the Sonlight Center, once the new Dalton hotel had been sited on the land they bought from Uncle Jeff, next to the yacht club. Dalton was happy, Caldwell Cove was happy with its new source of income, and Luke had found a job that would let him pay back a little of what had been done for him.

And, as if to round out her happiness, they were living back in Caldwell Cove, where she could use her skills at the inn and be a volunteer at the center. They were both doing things that mattered. They'd both come home.

"There." Gran opened the box she held and lifted out the creamy lace veil—the one Caldwell brides had worn since the first Chloe. It fluttered over Chloe's hair, light as an angel's wing. "Now you're ready."

She pushed the door open. Daniel stood ready to escort their mother, and David offered his arm to Gran with a gallant bow. Miranda started Sammy down the aisle with his precious cargo of wedding rings, then blew a kiss to Chloe as she took her place.

Her father held out his arm. "Ready, Chloe-girl?"

She slipped her hand into the crook of his arm, feeling his strength. She let her gaze drift across the small sanctuary, treasuring every inch of it. Even the bracket where the dolphin had stood was filled with the arrangement of beach roses and baby's breath that Miranda had put there.

Finally she looked at Luke. His eyes met hers, and she could see his love for her shining across the length of the church.

Thankfulness filled her soul. She squeezed her father's arm. "I'm ready," she said.

* * * * *

Be sure to watch for Matt's story,
coming in September to Love Inspired.
And now for a sneak preview of

A MOTHER'S WISH,

please turn the page.

It took him seconds to remind himself he was

Chapter One

If he had to go into exile for the next six months, Matt Caldwell couldn't have picked a better place than this. He paused outside the office of the *Caldwell Cove Gazette* and took a deep breath, inhaling the mixture of sea, salt and the rich musky aroma of the marshes. Home—Caldwell Cove, South Carolina. He'd know that distinctive smell in an instant no matter where he was on the globe. Quiet, peaceful—

Pop, pop, pop—a sharp sound broke the drowsy June silence. Matt's stomach lurched. He ducked in the response that had become second nature to him over the past few years, adrenaline pumping, fists clenching. He had to get everyone to cover.

Fragmented images shot through his mind. He smelled the acrid smoke of an explosion, felt the bone-jarring crash, heard the cries of children.

It took him seconds to remind himself he was in

Caldwell Cove, not on a bomb-ridden Indonesian street, seconds more to identify the sound. Some kid must be playing with caps in the lane beside the newspaper office.

A few quick strides took him around the side of the weathered gray building. Sure enough, that's what it was. The gut-wrenching fear subsided, to be replaced by anger. These boys were too young to be playing with caps. What kind of parents did they have, anyway?

"What are you doing?"

At his sharp question, two young faces looked up with startled expressions.

"We weren't doing anything." The speaker clasped his hands behind his back. His little brother nodded agreement, identical blue eyes round with surprise. "Honest."

Matt frowned at the word. *Honest* was the last thing the kid was being. "You were playing with caps. Don't you know that's dangerous? Where's your mother?" When they didn't answer, he planted his hands on his hips and glared, waiting. "Well?"

"I'm their mother." The woman flew around the corner as she spoke. She grabbed the boys and pulled them against her.

Matt looked into eyes the same shade of blue as the kids', sparkling with indignation. Her softly rounded face and curling brown hair reminded him of a Renaissance portrait, but her expression spoke more of a mother tiger, ready to protect her young.

"Why are you shouting at my sons?" She threw the words at him, sparking his anger.

"Maybe you'd shout, too, if you were paying attention to your own kids." He knew as he said the words he was going too far, but the emotions of the past few months still rode him, erasing normal politeness. "Or don't you care what they're up to?"

The woman's mouth tightened, and she looked as if she reviewed several things she might say before responding. "I can't imagine what concern my child rearing is to you."

"It isn't. But I have to care when I see kids in danger." He forced away the images that still haunted his dreams—of crying children huddled into makeshift bomb shelters or lying still on beds in crowded hospitals. "Your little angels were playing with caps."

"Caps?" That stopped her dead. She switched to the kids, looking into their faces with a hand on each one's shoulder. "Ethan? Jeffrey? Is that right?"

Matt waited for a quick denial again, but it didn't come. Apparently they had more trouble fibbing to her than to a stranger. The younger one looked down; the older one flushed and nodded.

"We didn't get hurt, Mommy."

"Ethan, that's not the point. You know better, both of you. Where did you get the caps?"

The kid looked as if he was searching for an appropriate answer and didn't find it. Finally he shrugged. "We found them. In that old shed back there.'' He pointed toward the rear of the building, where a tumbledown shed leaned against the next building.

''I told you...'' The woman stopped, and Matt saw the pink in her cheeks deepen. She probably didn't want to be having this discussion in front of him. ''Go to your room, both of you. Right now. We'll talk about this in a bit.''

The boys scampered around the building, and the woman looked as if she'd like to do the same. But she turned to face him, her color still high.

''I'm sorry.'' The words were stiff, making it clear she hadn't forgiven his sharp words. ''I appreciate your concern.''

He shrugged. ''It's nothing.'' He wanted to walk away and get on with his affairs, but the awkward moment seemed to demand something more. He was back in Caldwell Cove now. ''I'm Matt Caldwell, by the way.''

''Matt...'' Her eyes widened with what might have been surprise but looked more like shock. ''I should have recognized you. I'm Sarah Reed.''

Sarah Reed. Now he was the one left speechless. The woman he'd basically accused of being a careless mother was his new partner at the *Caldwell Cove Gazette.*

Dear Reader,

I'm so glad you decided to pick up this book. I've been longing to return to the Carolina coast that I love, so I'm especially happy to be writing the stories of the Caldwell kin—an extended family whose members learn the truth of the Scripture passages Gran Caldwell chose for each of them when they were baptized. I love stories about big families, and I hope you do, too.

Chloe Caldwell, the heroine of *Hunter's Bride*, has let Gran believe she's dating her boss, corporate executive Luke Hunter. Her charade explodes in her face when Gran invites Luke to Caldwell Cove for her eightieth birthday celebration. To her horror, Luke announces he'll attend as the beau Gran believes him to be. Luke and Chloe are convinced that their romance is just an act, but there are surprises in store for them when Chloe's loving, interfering family decides she should be the next Caldwell bride.

I'd love to hear from you and send you a signed bookplate or bookmark. Please write to me:
Marta Perry, c/o Steeple Hill Books, 300 East 42nd St., Sixth Floor, New York, New York 10017.

Marta Perry